CUCINA LEGGERA

Light & Healthy
Recipes from Northern Italy

BY ANDREA DODI WITH EMILY DODI
ILLUSTRATED BY JENNIE OPPENHEIMER

HPBooks
a division of
PRICE STERN SLOAN
Los Angeles

Published by HPBooks
a division of Price Stern Sloan, Inc.
11150 Olympic Boulevard, Sixth Floor
Los Angeles, CA 90064

©1992 Andrea Dodi
Illustrations ©1992 Price Stern Sloan

ISBN: 1-55788-048-4
Printed in the United States of America

10 9 8 7 6 5 4 3 2 1

This book is printed on acid-free paper.

Dedication

To our family, on both sides of the Atlantic.

Dear Reader,

Before you indulge in the lightest, most delicious offerings from the land where food is king, please take note of the following changes to a few recipes:

Polenta with Broccoli and Gorgonzola Cheese (page 100)

4 cups water must be used, not 2.

Ice Cream Delight (page 151)

1/4 Cup *brewed* Espresso Coffee (or American Coffee), not coffee grounds, must be used.

Cold Rice Salad (page 4)
(Another, Preferred Option)

Add rice to 6 cups boiling water. Cook 10-12 minutes, or until rice is tender, strain like pasta.

Thank you for picking up a copy of **Cucina Leggera**, and we hope it brings you countless memories of fine food and special times.

Buon Appetito e Lunga Vita!

Table of Contents

Salve (Greeting) viii

Consigli (Words of Advice) ix

Antipasti e Insalate (Appetizers & Salads) 1

Zuppe (Soups) 15

Pesce (Fish & Shellfish)..29

Pollame e Uove (Poultry & Eggs) 43

Carne (Beef, Lamb, Pork & Veal)......................................65

Pasta 77

Polenta e Riso (Polenta & Rice)..97

Focaccie, Gnocchi, Pane e Pisarei
    (Breads & Dumplings)...109

Verdure (Vegetables) 119

Salse (Sauces & Garnishes) 131

Dolci (Desserts)..147

Italian Recipe List 116

Index...163

Acknowledgments

Many thanks to Laura and Jeanette for all their patience and encouragement.

To the many people I have had the pleasure of sharing wonderful food with over the years, I give my thanks. And to Mr. and Mrs. Bill Koch, who inspired me to cook light and healthy.

—Andrea

Many thanks to Laura, who envisioned a wonderful book and made it happen. To Jeanette and Bret, for all their hard work—it is very much appreciated.

Thanks to all my friends who were generous food critics.

To Ann, whose support and advice made all the difference. And to Mike, who wasn't afraid to offer honest criticism, even in the middle of the night or when I was wielding sharp kitchen utensils.

—Emily

Salve

Greeting

My career as a chef began forty years ago in Paris, but my education in food began seventy years ago in the small Northern Italian town of Pitolo, outside of Piacenza in the Emilia-Romagna Province. It was there I watched my mother and sisters prepare simple peasant food for our family of eleven. Polenta, soups, breads, dumplings, rice and beans covered our table even during the toughest times. The meals were simple and filling—delicious even though made from the most basic ingredients.

After the World War II, like so many young Italians, I left in search of a better life. I moved to Paris and there my love and knowledge of food blossomed. Where I had learned the true grit of cooking from the women of my family, I now learned the finer touches and finesse of French cuisine from great Parisian chefs and from Denise, the woman who would become my wife.

Denise and I moved to America in 1950 and again my education took on greater dimensions. Fine hostesses such as Mary Lasker, Irene Selznick, Marion Javitz, Joan Fontaine and Dorothy Killgallen, among others, taught me about the tastes and preferences of the people for whom I still cook today. My clients continue to teach me about food. Beginning in the mid-1980s, I saw that they desired lowfat, low-cholesterol cooking, so I learned how to give them delicious, authentic and light Italian cuisine.

This book embodies my lifelong education in food and is meant to give other cooks a quick and easy education in preparing classic light and healthy Northern Italian recipes, as well as many of my own. Imagine, twenty years ago I didn't even know how to prepare light dishes because no one had ever requested them. I had to learn, just as you have, to cook healthier meals. Today it is the only way I will cook, at home and at parties.

My recipes are simple to follow, and my hints and shortcuts will help you master the dishes in no time. But remember, the more you make a dish, the better it will taste. My daughter Emily can testify to that. Following a recipe exactly is just part of creating a perfect dish: it also takes confidence and intuition that will only come with experience. In time, just as I have done, you will add more and more of your own favorite herbs and ingredients to make each dish your own creation.

Consigli

Words of Advice

Terms & Techniques

Al Dente: Pasta, rice and vegetables are best when prepared *al dente*. This means cooked until tender, but still chewy, not mushy or soft.

Antipasti (Appetizers): Literally means "before the pasta." Keep them light and lowfat. Don't fill your guests up on heavy tidbits before the main course is served.

Kneading: For most of the recipes in this book, knead dough by hand. (It's a lot more fun!) Have at least 1/4-cup flour covering the kneading surface and dust your hands with flour as well. Use the heel of your hand to push against the dough to stretch it gently, then bring the dough forward with your fingers. Rotate the dough slightly as you repeat the movements. Don't over-knead; five or six times is enough for most recipes in this book.

Perfect Timing: This is the last thing I mastered as a chef. Read every recipe in a menu ahead of time and decide in which order to prepare the dishes. Prepare items which take a long time to cook, or that can be reheated, first. Quick recipes can be made last. All it takes is a little planning and a cool head to get everything ready on time.

Ingredients

Bacon & Bacon Substitutes: Use leaner bacon or bacon substitutes made from turkey or lean beef when a favorite recipe cannot be made without something resembling the normally high-fat meat.

Basil: Bruising basil is called for in many Italian recipes. Gently press fresh basil leaves with a kitchen mallet until they become dark.

Bread Crumbs: Recipes in this book use coarse, rather than fine, plain and Italian-flavored bread crumbs. If you use fine bread crumbs, reduce the amount called for in the recipe, as they pack more tightly in the cup. If you purchase bread crumbs, try different brands until you find the one you like.

Cantaloupe: To this day I can't pick out a ripe cantaloupe as well as my wife Denise. A good rule to go by is its color and smell. It shouldn't be too green or too yellow, and too strong a smell means the cantaloupe is too ripe—it should have a slightly sweet aroma.

Cheese: Look for lowfat, low-cholesterol versions of traditional choices. Buy ricotta and mozzarella cheeses made from skim or part-skim milk. Read labels carefully. Cheeses such as Parmesan are high in fat, but just a little adds a lot of flavor.

Dried Mushrooms: Different varieties of dried mushrooms are available. They all need to be soaked in water before using—the length of time will vary depending on how long they are to be cooked.

Garlic & Onions: Please don't keep these in the refrigerator. The best place for garlic is in a ceramic jug with holes. Keep onions in a hanging basket in a dry, cool place. Refrigeration will rob them of flavor.

Herbs: Oregano, marjoram and basil are typical Italian herbs. When using dried herbs instead of fresh, substitute one-fourth to one-third the amount called for in the recipe and when substituting fresh herbs for dried ones, use three to four times the amount. When a recipe calls for fresh rosemary, grind it for a few seconds in a food processor, or chop it up by hand. This will release more flavor.

Liquid Egg Substitutes: There are several brands available of this no-cholesterol, pasteurized egg product. Use when just egg whites won't do in a recipe. Salt is usually added during processing, so do not over-salt the dish.

Nonstick Cooking Spray: This makes greasing your pans quick and easy, and reduces the amount of calories from fat.

Pasta: All types of pasta must be cooked in enough water to cover. For best results, add 1 to 2 tablespoons of olive or vegetable oil and a pinch of salt to the pot before water boils. The oil will prevent pasta from clumping together, while the salt will add flavor and make the water boil faster. The only no-fault way to tell whether pasta is done is to taste it!

Polenta: Look for precooked polenta available in stores to save you the labor and time that homemade polenta requires.

Equipment

Blender: An useful tool to blend sauces and soups.

Food Processor: Get one if you don't already have one. It will make recipe preparation infinitely easier. Small or mini ones are good for processing small amounts of ingredients. A large food processor can be used for pureeing soups and making bread and pasta.

Mortar: The word may conjure up images of the Middle Ages or the world's first pharmacists, but mortars—those stone bowls used with pestles—continue to be extremely useful in crushing foods and are a must in every chef's kitchen. They are especially helpful when making a small amount of ingredients into a paste.

Nonstick Pans & Skillets: These allow you to use less fat in cooking and make cleanup a breeze. Invest in quality products.

Rubber Spatula: Worth the meager investment—buy several, this tool will make your cooking infinitely simpler, and is the one utensil I use most often.

Wooden Spoon: A valuable tool that no authentic Italian kitchen should be without.

Antipasti e Insalate

Appetizers & Salads

These two dishes have gone through as many revolutionary changes as today's main courses. Adopting a lower fat and cholesterol content is only part of the transformation.

Years ago, my staff and I would work hours just to prepare the appetizers for a party of as few as twenty people. Favorite appetizers of the day were laden with cream sauces or baked in buttery puff pastry. Today, appetizers, as with main courses, follow one simple rule: the lighter and easier to make, the better. No one wants to fill up on heavy appetizers before a delicious meal, and you should never have to spend hours in the kitchen preparing them like I had to do in the old days.

Salads follow trends, too. Today, cooks are eager to experiment. They are trying out ingredients from all over the world and using unusual vegetables to add dimension, color and new flavors to their cooking. Where we once opted for simple salads made with Bibb, Boston or Romaine lettuce, we're now more adventurous. These days, radicchio, endive and arugala, among other once-exotic ingredients, are showing up on more and more American dinner tables. The salads I have chosen feature many of these ingredients, as well as some of the most popular salad ingredients from my home region of Italy.

Mozzarella, Tomato & Basil Salad

Insalata di Mozzarella, Pomodori e Basilico

Serves: 8
Preparation Time: 15 minutes
Cooking Time: 0

15 ounces part-skim mozzarella cheese
6 ripe Roma tomatoes
10 fresh basil leaves
2 tablespoons extra-virgin olive oil
Freshly ground pepper to taste
2 tablespoons balsamic vinegar (optional)

This is a classic salad served at every self-respecting Italian restaurant. At home, regular mozzarella cheese will work nicely, but for real perfection go to a specialty shop and purchase buffalo mozzarella.

Slice mozzarella cheese into 1/4-inch rounds and set aside. Slice tomatoes into 1/4-inch rounds. Wash basil leaves and dry well. On a platter, arrange mozzarella cheese, tomatoes and basil in alternate layers. Just before serving, drizzle with olive oil and sprinkle with pepper. If using vinegar, combine with the olive oil in a small bowl before pouring over the salad. Serve cool or at room temperature.

All'Italiana: The best way to enjoy this classic salad is by arranging every ingredient on a thick slice of Italian bread. The mozzarella cheese will be creamy, the tomatoes sweet and the basil will add a subtle fragrance.

Per Serving:
Calories: 88   Total Fat: 6 g   Sat. Fat: 2 g   Chol.: 10 mg

Italian Bean Salad with Tuna

Insalata di Fagioli

Serves: 4 to 6
Preparation Time: 30 minutes including refrigeration time
Cooking Time: 0

Perfect for picnics or as a light dinner, this ideal summer dish doesn't require slaving in a hot kitchen.

2 (15-oz.) cans pinto or white beans (4 cups)
1 medium-size onion, chopped
1 garlic clove, chopped
1 red bell pepper, chopped
1 tablespoon olive oil
1 tablespoon parsley, chopped
1 (6-1/8-oz.) can white albacore tuna packed in oil
Salt and black pepper to taste
1 head Boston lettuce

Rinse beans in a colander under running water until water runs clear. Drain thoroughly. In a large bowl, combine all ingredients, except lettuce. Mix gently until tuna is in tiny pieces. Do not crush beans. Refrigerate 1/2 hour. Rinse and dry lettuce. Arrange lettuce leaves on individual salad plates, top with bean mixture and serve.

Variations: To use fresh green beans, cook over medium heat in enough water to cover 10 to 15 minutes, or until tender. Drain and let beans cool before combining with other ingredients. To use uncooked dried beans, follow package directions. This dish looks wonderful in a salad bowl on its own—so serve without lettuce, if you so desire.

All'Italiana: This dish is very popular in Venice during the summer months, and is served frequently at open-air markets and festivals where people want substantial food, but nothing heavy or hot.

Per Serving:
Calories: 315   Total Fat: 8 g   Sat. Fat: 1 g   Chol.: 8 mg

Cold Rice Salad

Riso Freddo

Serves: 4
Preparation Time: 15 minutes plus 1 hour cooling time
Cooking Time: 20 to 25 minutes

3 cups water
3/4 teaspoon salt
1-1/2 cups short-grain rice
1/4 teaspoon pepper
1 tablespoon red wine vinegar
Juice from 2 lemons
1 tablespoon capers
12 large pitted ripe olives, chopped
1 (6-1/8-oz.) can white albacore tuna packed in oil
1/2 red bell pepper, chopped
1/2 green bell pepper, chopped
1/2 cup light mayonnaise
1 ripe tomato, sliced
1/2 cucumber, sliced
1/2 red bell pepper, sliced
1/2 green bell pepper, sliced

At your next picnic, toss the soggy potato salad aside for this Mediterranean treat.

In a large pan over medium heat, bring the 3 cups salted water to a boil. Add rice. Boil 12 to 14 minutes until rice is tender, but slightly chewy (al dente). Reduce heat if water begins to boil over edge of pan. Drain rice through a colander and place in a large serving bowl. Mix in salt, pepper, vinegar, lemon juice and capers. Let stand 1 hour at room temperature. Stir in olives, tuna in its oil, chopped bell peppers and mayonnaise. Garnish with remaining ingredients and serve.

All'Italiana: This is meant to be enjoyed *al fresco*. Slice some good Italian bread and have several other salads or cold dishes on the table for a perfect summer supper.

Per Serving:
Calories: 374   Total Fat: 11 g   Sat. Fat: 0.4 g   Chol.: 10 mg

Italian Eggplant Salad

Insalata di Melanzane

Serves: 6
Preparation Time: 12 minutes plus 1 hour for standing and cooling
Cooking Time: 5 to 10 minutes

2 medium-size Italian eggplants
1/2 cup coarse kosher salt
1/4 cup olive oil
1 garlic clove
Pepper to taste
1/2 cup red wine vinegar

Imagine a sunny veranda overlooking the Mediterranean and cypress trees rustling in the wind. Now picture a beautifully set table. Look closely and you will see this popular salad.

Remove tops and ends from eggplants. Do not peel. Cut eggplants lengthwise into 1/4-inch slices. Arrange slices in 1 layer on 3 paper towels. Sprinkle eggplant slices liberally with kosher salt. Combine olive oil and garlic in a small bowl. Let both eggplant and olive oil mixture stand 30 minutes. Remove garlic from olive oil and discard. Pat eggplant slices dry and brush off salt. Brush 1 side of eggplant slices with olive oil. In a large nonstick skillet over medium heat, lay as many eggplant slices as will fit, with the oiled side facing down. Sprinkle with pepper. Cook 2 minutes. Brush top of slices with olive oil and turn over. Cook 2 minutes more, or until eggplant slices have lost their greenish tint on both sides and the edges are slightly turned up. Repeat until all eggplant slices are cooked. Remove from heat and sprinkle with additional pepper and vinegar. Let cool 30 minutes and serve.

Variation: Table salt may be used instead of coarse kosher salt.

All'Italiana: Great as a supplement to any salad plate, or incredible in a sandwich. Combine eggplant slices with Italian peppers or Italian meatballs! *Delizioso!*

Per Serving:
Calories: 103   Total Fat: 9 g   Sat. Fat: 1 g   Chol.: 0 mg

5

Mushrooms with Lemon & Oil

Funghi Crudi al Limone e Olio

Serves: 8
Preparation Time: 15 minutes plus 2 hours standing time
Cooking Time: 0

1 pound white mushrooms
1 teaspoon salt
2 tablespoons extra-virgin olive oil
1 lemon
1 teaspoon white pepper

A young Sardinian housekeeper taught me how to fix this delectable vegetarian dish that is a Southern Italian classic. I may be straying from the North, but I have to share this with you—it's one of my favorites!

Rinse mushrooms well and slice very thin. In a colander, sprinkle salt over mushrooms. Place 2 paper towels over mushrooms and place bowl on top. This will help squeeze out excess water from mushrooms. Let stand 2 hours at room temperature. Place mushrooms in a medium-size bowl and add oil. Cut lemon in half and squeeze juice from both halves over mushrooms. Taste for saltiness and add if needed. Add white pepper, stir to combine and serve.

All'Italiana: The best way to serve this dish is to spoon it onto lightly toasted slices of Italian bread.

Per Serving:
Calories: 45 g   Total Fat: 4 g   Sat. Fat: 0.5 g   Chol.: 0 mg

Sardine & Anchovy Spread

Burro di Acciughe e Sardine

Serves: 8 to 10
Preparation Time: 5 minutes
Cooking Time: 0

3 to 4 ounces boneless sardines
10 to 13 anchovy fillets
1 teaspoon lemon juice
6 ounces reduced-fat cream
    cheese (3/4 cup)
1 tablespoon cognac

Give tuna a rest. Utilize the "other" canned fish, which so many Americans shy away from, to make a distinctive Italian antipasti.

Remove bones from sardines, if not already boned. In a blender or food processor equipped with the metal blade, process all ingredients until they form a thick paste.

All'Italiana: Serve this delectable spread on thin toasted slices of Italian bread. Or go American, and dish it up on a celery stalk or rye cracker.

Per Serving:
Calories: 93   *Total Fat: 7 g*   *Sat. Fat: 3 g*   *Chol.: 36 mg*

Smoked Salmon Spread

Burro di Salmone

Serves: 8 to 10
Preparation Time: 10 minutes
Cooking Time: 0

1/2 pound smoked salmon
4 ounces reduced-fat cream
    cheese (1/2 cup)
1/4 teaspoon crushed dried dill
    weed
1 pinch of freshly ground
    pepper
15 to 20 rye crackers
1/2 lemon (optional), thinly
    sliced

This recipe has been a favorite of mine for over forty years, and clients ask for it again and again.

In a blender or food processor equipped with the metal blade, process all ingredients except crackers and lemon until they form a thick paste. Serve in a small bowl surrounded by crackers. Garnish with several thin slices of lemon, if desired.

Variation: Feel free to use your favorite crackers or toasted thin rounds of French bread.

All'Italiana: This a perfect prelude to Risotto Milanese (page 103) or any other hearty risotto dish.

Per Serving:
Calories: 112   Total Fat: 4 g   Sat. Fat: 2 g   Chol.: 18 mg

Stuffed Endive Leaves

Foglie di Indivia con Burro di Noci

Serves: 10 to 12
Preparation Time: 5 minutes
Cooking Time: 0

5 heads of Belgian endive
1/2 cup unsalted almonds
1/2 cup unsalted pecans
1/2 cup unsalted hazelnuts
   (filberts)
1/2 cup unsalted roasted
   peanuts

A delightful nutty flavor adds panache to delicate endive leaves. Bellissima!

Separate and rinse endive leaves. Set aside to dry. In a food processor equipped with the metal blade, or with a mortar and pestle, process nuts until they form a thick paste. Pat endive leaves dry and fill lightly with nut paste.

All'Italiana: This appetizer works best at the table, but it can also be served on a tray as finger food. An Orvieto or Pinot Grigio wine complement this dish perfectly.

Per Serving:
Calories: 129   Total Fat: 12 g   Sat. Fat: 2 g   Chol.: 0 mg

Baked Mozzarella

Mozzarella in Forno

Serves: 6
Preparation Time: 7 minutes
Cooking Time: 15 to 20 minutes

8 ounces part-skim mozzarella cheese
6 egg whites
1/2 cup all-purpose flour
2 cups coarse Italian seasoned bread crumbs, crushed
2 tablespoons olive oil

This gooey treat was a hit at the Italian Consulate in New York. It made such a splash that it was requested at every other dinner I catered for them.

Preheat oven to 400F (205C). Cut cheese into 1-inch cubes. In a bowl, beat egg whites until foamy. In another bowl, combine flour and bread crumbs. Dip each cheese cube into egg whites, then into flour mixture until well coated. Dip again into egg whites and roll one more time in flour mixture. Squeeze each cheese cube gently in palm of hand to assure that coating is firmly attached. Arrange cheese on a nonstick baking sheet. Drizzle with olive oil. Bake about 5 minutes, or until brown. Serve hot with a wooden pick in each cube.

Variation: Now mozzarella cheese is available in fun strips or strings. Use strips whole, or cut a strip into smaller pieces.

All'Italiana: My daughter Emily just opens a jar of store-bought tomato sauce, heats it up in the microwave and serves it as a dip for the hot cheese cubes.

Per Serving:
Calories: 211   Total Fat: 11 g   Sat. Fat: 4 g   Chol.: 21 mg

Zucchini with Bread Crumbs

Zucchini con Pangrattato

Serves: 10
Preparation Time: 5 minutes
Cooking Time: 3 to 5 minutes

2 tablespoons olive oil
3 cups sliced zucchini (1/4 inch thick)
1/4 teaspoon salt
1/4 teaspoon pepper
3 tablespoons coarse plain bread crumbs, crushed
2 tablespoons grated Parmesan cheese
1/2 teaspoon garlic powder

This is one of my calling cards. It works well at any type of party, from a casual get-together to a formal sit-down dinner.

In a large nonstick skillet over medium heat, heat olive oil. Add zucchini and cook 3 to 5 minutes, or until zucchini becomes a bit translucent and slightly brown on the edges, turning as needed. Remove from heat. Add salt, pepper, bread crumbs, Parmesan cheese and garlic powder. Toss well. Serve in a basket lined with waxed paper or as individual appetizers pierced with wooden picks on a tray.

All'Italiana: Serve this pleaser with a small dish of Dill Mayonnaise (page 139) on the side for dunking.

Per Serving:
Calories: 43   *Total Fat: 3 g*   *Sat. Fat: 0.6 g*   *Chol.: 1 mg*

Fish Rolls

Sogliole Infagottate

Serves: 4 to 6
Preparation Time: 15 minutes
Cooking Time: 12 to 15 minutes

2 tablespoons finely chopped celery
2 tablespoons finely chopped onion
1 tablespoon dried leaf parsley
1/4 teaspoon dried leaf thyme
1 pinch of dried leaf marjoram
2 tablespoons olive oil
1 cup coarse plain bread crumbs, crushed
1/2 pound sole (1 to 3 fillets)
1 tablespoon grated Parmesan cheese

Dip:
1 cup Tofunetta (page 132)
1/2 cup crumbled Gorgonzola cheese (2 ounces)

I remember making this dish many years ago for Senator and Mrs. Jacob Javitz. Their parties were always a lot of fun to cater because they invited so many notable figures, including Henry Kissinger.

Spray a shallow nonstick baking pan with nonstick cooking spray. Preheat broiler. In a large bowl, combine vegetables, herbs, olive oil and bread crumbs. Rinse and pat dry sole fillets. Lay out fillets on a work surface. Spread a thin layer of vegetable mixture evenly over fillets. Gently roll each fillet tightly. Place them side by side in prepared baking pan. Sprinkle with Parmesan cheese. Broil 12 to 15 minutes, or until golden-brown. To test for doneness, test fillets at thickest part with a fork. Fish should be white, not translucent or shiny. Prepare dip. Cut fillets into 1-inch thick rolls. Pour dip into a small serving bowl and arrange fish rolls around bowl and serve with wooden picks.

Dip
In a small bowl, combine Tofunetta and Gorgonzola cheese.

Variation: Instead of Tofunetta, use 1 cup plain nonfat yogurt.

All'Italiana: I prefer to serve this before a summer meal of Cold Rice Salad (page 4) or Italian Bean Salad with Tuna (page 3).

Per Serving:
Calories: 293   Total Fat: 14 g   Sat. Fat: 4 g   Chol.: 42 mg

Eggplant Appetizer

Caponata

Serves: 6
Preparation Time: 10 minutes plus 2 hours refrigeration time
Cooking Time: 20 minutes

1 large Italian eggplant
2 tablespoons olive oil
2 medium-size onions, coarsely chopped
1 red bell pepper, coarsely chopped
1 green bell pepper, coarsely chopped
3 garlic cloves
1 cup canned whole tomatoes
8 pitted green olives
8 pitted ripe olives
2 tablespoons capers
1/4 cup red wine vinegar
1/4 teaspoon sugar

I made this for Irene Selznick when she was producing "A Street Car Named Desire." Her guest lists read like a who's who of Hollywood.

Peel eggplant and cut into 1/2-inch cubes. In a large non-stick skillet over medium heat, heat olive oil. Add eggplant and sauté 2 minutes on each side. Transfer eggplant to a large bowl and set aside. In a food processor equipped with the metal blade, process onions, bell peppers, garlic, tomatoes and olives 10 seconds, or until coarsely chopped. Add vegetable mixture to the same large skillet over low heat and simmer 10 minutes. Stir in eggplant and capers. Cook 1 minute and remove from heat. In a small saucepan over medium heat, bring vinegar and sugar to a boil, stirring to dissolve sugar. Pour over eggplant mixture and refrigerate 2 hours. Serve cold.

All'Italiana: Caponata is classic Italian fare. Serve it cold and scoop it up with bits of Romaine lettuce or thin slices of Italian bread.

Per Serving:
Calories: 110   Total Fat: 6 g   Sat. Fat: 1 g   Chol.: 0 mg

Zuppe

Soups

The recipes in this chapter reach far back into my childhood. They are, for the most part, hearty peasant soups I learned from my mother. Growing up, soup was a very important part of my family's meals. Because food was sparse during our toughest times, soup sustained us with its hearty broths, delicate herbs, fresh vegetables and delicious pasta or rice. Here are my favorite recipes from my mother's kitchen, as well as my own. Although they are filling, the best part about these soups is that they are naturally low in fat and cholesterol, or have been altered to be such without losing their rich taste and texture. They are simple to make and, except for the minestrone, all are ready to serve in about an hour. Many utilize root vegetables such as turnips, onions and carrots, as well as beans, making them a great source of protein and fiber. They will warm you and make you feel good. They've always done the trick for me.

Rice & Chickpea Soup

Zuppa di Riso e Ceci

Serves: 6
Preparation Time: 10 minutes
Cooking Time: 15 minutes

10 large spinach leaves
2 garlic cloves
1 small red onion
3 cups cooked chickpeas
  (garbanzos)
6 cups water
3/4 cup short-grain rice
1 tablespoon dried leaf basil
1 teaspoon dried leaf thyme

A quick-to-fix, sure-to-please soup. It's hearty enough to be a meal on its own.

Wash spinach and remove stems. In a food processor equipped with the metal blade, or by hand, chop garlic, onion, half of the spinach and half of the chickpeas together until fine but not mushy. Set aside. In a large pan, bring water to a boil. Add chopped ingredients and rice. (Don't let the green foam discourage you, it will disappear). Cover and simmer over medium heat 10 minutes, or until onion is cooked. Add remaining chickpeas and spinach leaves and herbs and simmer 3 more minutes. Pour into soup bowls. Serve hot.

Variations: Use 1/4 cup fresh basil instead of dried basil. For a heartier soup, use 4 cups water and 2 cups chicken broth. Also, large dark green lettuce leaves (such as romaine) can be substituted for spinach.

Hint: Serve this soup quickly, because the longer it stands the more water the rice will absorb and it will begin to resemble risotto and not soup.

All'Italiana: Add grated Parmesan cheese. But beware, heaping Parmesan cheese will load on the cholesterol and fat. Go easy, but indulge like a true Italian—just a little.

Per Serving:
Calories: 131   Total Fat: 0.6 g   Sat. Fat: 0 g   Chol.: 0 mg

Three Pepper Soup

Zuppa di Peperoni

Serves: 4
Preparation Time: 15 minutes
Cooking Time: 17 minutes

1 small yellow bell pepper,
    coarsely chopped
1 small red bell pepper,
    coarsely chopped
1 medium-size onion
1 large green bell pepper
1 small russet potato
1-1/2 cups chicken broth
1-1/2 cups water
Salt and black pepper to taste
1/4 cup Tofunetta (page 132)
    (optional)

I prepared this soup at an elegant party in Greece for Henry Ford II. A gorgeous green soup, I garnished it with dollops of red and yellow pepper purees. It was a hit!

In a blender set to high speed or a small food processor equipped with the metal blade, puree yellow bell pepper 15 seconds, or until smooth. Spoon into a small bowl. Set aside. Rinse out blender or processor. Repeat with red bell pepper. Set aside. Chop remaining vegetables into tiny bite-size pieces. In a large pan over low heat, simmer chopped vegetables in chicken broth and water 15 minutes, or until vegetables are tender. Season with salt and pepper. Stir in Tofunetta if a creamier texture is desired and simmer 2 minutes, or until hot. Do not boil. Spoon into serving bowls and add a dollop each of red and yellow bell pepper purees on top of soup.

All'Italiana: Italians love garlic and spices, but with a dish like this, the true flavor of the delicious vegetables are left untouched and uncomplicated. *Perfetto.*

Per Serving:
Calories: 90   Total Fat: 1 g   Sat. Fat: 0.2 g   Chol.: 1 mg

Creamy Carrot Soup

Zuppa di Carote e Tofunetta

Serves: 6
Preparation Time: 15 minutes
Cooking Time: 25 minutes

1 pound carrots, sliced
1 medium-size russet potato, sliced
1 large onion, sliced
2 cups water
2 chicken bouillon cubes
1 cup Tofunetta (page 132)
Skim milk, if needed

A creamy golden delight that's sure to please everyone.

In a large pan over medium heat, cook carrots, potato and onion in water 18 minutes. Add bouillon cubes and Tofunetta. Cook 2 minutes. In a blender set to high speed or a food processor equipped with the metal blade, process soup until smooth. If soup is too thick for your taste, add a little skim milk at a time and process until it reaches the desired consistency. Return to pan and simmer over low heat until hot.

Variation: Use 2 vegetable bouillon cubes in place of chicken bouillon cubes.

All'Italiana: Don't waste a drop of this soup. Soak up the last bit with Italian bread.

Per Serving:
Calories: 106   Total Fat: 2 g   Sat. Fat: 0.3 g   Chol.: 0 mg

Chickpea Soup

Zuppa di Ceci

Serves: 8
Preparation Time: 15 minutes plus overnight soaking time
Cooking Time: 2 to 3 hours

1/4 cup olive oil
1 cup coarsely chopped celery
1 cup coarsely chopped carrot
1 medium-size onion, coarsely chopped
2 cups dried chickpeas (garbonzos), soaked overnight
About 2 quarts water
Salt and pepper to taste

Sure to soothe you with warmth. Mother was right, soup can fix almost anything.

In a large pan over medium heat, heat olive oil. Add celery, carrot and onion and sauté 5 minutes. Add chickpeas. Add enough water to reach 2 inches above ingredients. Cover and simmer over low heat 2 to 3 hours, or until chickpeas are very tender. Season with salt and pepper. Serve hot.

Varitaion: The same amount of canned chickpeas can work just as well. Rinse and drain them before adding to soup.

All'Italiana: Here is an opportunity for you to experiment with your favorite Italian herbs. Start with one teaspoon of a dried herb and add more as desired.

Per Serving:
Calories: 265   Total Fat: 9 g   Sat. Fat: 1 g   Chol.: 0 mg

19

Turnip Soup

Zuppa di Ravanelli

Serves: 4 to 6
Preparation Time: 15 minutes
Cooking Time: 20 to 25 minutes

2 medium-size turnips
1 medium-size potato
2 cups water
1 chicken bouillon cube
3/4 cup Tofunetta (page 132)
1/2 cup crumbled Gorgonzola
   cheese (2 ounces)

If turnips haven't made it to your dinner table yet, this soup will make them a featured attraction from now on.

Chop vegetables into 1/8-inch cubes. In a large pan over medium heat, cook vegetables in water with bouillon cube 15 to 20 minutes, or until tender. Stir in Tofunetta. Simmer 5 minutes, or until hot (do not boil). Ladle into serving dishes and sprinkle with Gorgonzola cheese.

Variations: Use 12 ounces of canned or homemade chicken broth instead of bouillon cube; reduce water to 1/2 cup. You can serve the soup without the Gorgonzola cheese.

All'Italiana: This is a typical peasant soup, but one that can be transformed into an elegant dish if pureed to a creamy consistency.

Per Serving:
Calories: 129   Total Fat: 6 g   Sat. Fat: 4 g   Chol.:14 mg

Onion & Squash Soup

Zuppa di Cipolle e Zucche

Serves: 6
Preparation Time: 10 minutes
Cooking Time: 20 minutes

1-1/2 cups chicken broth
3 cups water
3 medium-size onions,
   chopped
2 cups chopped acorn squash
1/4 teaspoon salt
1/4 teaspoon pepper
1 pinch of nutmeg
1/2 cup nonfat plain yogurt

Savory! This is the perfect soup for a fall or winter dinner.

In a large pan over medium heat, bring chicken broth and water to a boil. Add onions and squash. Reduce heat and simmer 15 minutes, or until vegetables are tender. Remove from heat and let stand 3 minutes. Stir in salt, pepper and nutmeg. Simmer over low heat 2 minutes, then stir in yogurt and serve.

Note: Nutmeg is an especially strong-tasting spice—make your pinch a tiny one.

All'Italiana: A beautiful soup, it makes for a delicious prelude to a delicate fish dinner.

Per Serving:
Calories: 40   Total Fat: 1 g   Sat. Fat: 0.2 g   Chol.: 0 mg

Red Cabbage Soup

Zuppa di Cavolo Nero

Serves: 4
Preparation Time: 15 minutes
Cooking Time: 30 to 35 minutes

3 tablespoons olive oil
1 small onion, chopped
1 small white potato, quartered
1-1/2 cups beef broth
3 cups water
1-1/2 cups chopped red cabbage
2 medium-size carrots, sliced into rounds
1/4 teaspoon dried leaf marjoram
1/4 teaspoon dried leaf oregano
1 cup Classic Tomato Sauce (page 141) or purchased tomato pasta sauce
2 tablespoons grated Parmesan cheese (optional)

Italy's answer to borscht! A beautiful, impressive soup to serve to special guests, including your family!

In a large pan over medium heat, heat olive oil. Add onion and potato and sauté 5 to 10 minutes, or until onion is translucent. Add beef broth, water, cabbage, carrots, herbs and tomato sauce. Reduce heat and simmer 25 minutes, or until potato and carrots are tender enough to be mashed with a fork. Pour into soup bowls and sprinkle with Parmesan cheese, if desired. Serve hot or cold.

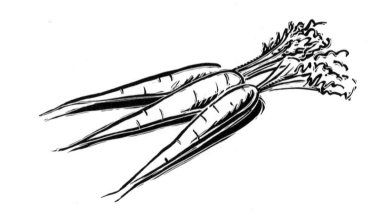

All'Italiana: What makes this borscht distinctively Italian? The herbs and delicate flavor of Parmesan cheese are the definitive Italian touches.

Per Serving:
Calories: 195   Total Fat: 12 g   Sat. Fat: 2 g   Chol.: 3 mg

Andrea's Minestrone

Minestrone di Andrea

Serves: 6
Preparation Time: 30 minutes
Cooking Time: 2-1/2 hours

About 1 pound lean beef short
  ribs
2 quarts water
2 large ripe tomatoes, peeled
  and seeded, or 2
  tablespoons tomato paste
2 large carrots, diced
2 medium-size celery stalks,
  chopped
1 cup fresh or frozen green peas
1 cup 1/2-inch pieces fresh
  green beans
1 small head of escarole, shredded
1 cup fresh spinach, stems
  removed and leaves
  shredded
3 medium-sized zucchini, diced
2 medium-sized potatoes
Salt and pepper to taste
1 teaspoon dried leaf oregano
10 fresh basil leaves (optional)
1/4 cup freshly-grated Parmesan
  cheese
1 tablespoon red wine vinegar
  (optional)

All'Italiana: Serve with

additional Parmesan cheese

on the side, and thick slices of

Italian bread for dunking.

This is one of my favorite soups to enjoy on its own as a nice hot lunch. As this is a slow-cooking dish, it will make your kitchen warm and fragrant.

Remove as much of the fat from the meat as possible, but do not remove bones. In a large pan, bring water to a boil. Add meat, tomatoes, carrots, celery, peas, beans, escarole, spinach and zucchini. Peel potatoes, but leave them whole, and add to soup. Cover and simmer over low heat 1 hour. Season with salt and pepper. Add oregano and simmer another hour, or until meat comes away from bones easily. Remove beef and debone. Discard bones and any gristle. Cut meat into bite-size pieces, then return to broth. If potatoes have not yet disintegrated, mash them with a fork in broth. Add basil and Parmesan cheese. Taste. If carrots and tomatoes have made the soup too sweet for your taste, add vinegar. Simmer 10 minutes longer and serve hot.

Variation: Feel free to substitute other vegetables, but be sure to use ones in the same family and keep the amounts the same. It's your soup, so add what you like best.

Per Serving:
Calories: 370   Total Fat: 16 g   Sat. Fat: 7 g   Chol.: 74 mg

Simple Soup

Stracciatella

Serves: 4
Preparation Time: 5 minutes
Cooking Time: 7 to 10 minutes

2 cups chicken broth
3 egg whites
2 tablespoons grated Parmesan cheese
1 tablespoon chopped parsley
Salt and pepper to taste

Every culture has its soothing version of chicken soup. The Italian one is simple to make and gives all the comfort of those other labor-intensive varieties.

In a medium-size pan over high heat, bring broth to a boil. Reduce heat and add other ingredients. Stir well with a whisk 2 minutes, then simmer 2 more minutes. Do not boil. Serve hot.

Variation: Beef broth can be used instead of chicken broth for a completely different flavor.

All'Italiana: Serve with hearty peasant bread for a delicious and completely satisfying lunch.

Per Serving:
Calories: 47   Total Fat: 2 g   Sat. Fat: 1 g   Chol.: 3 mg

Julia's Soup

Zuppa di Giulia

Serves: 4
Preparation Time: 10 minutes
Cooking Time: 25 minutes

2 medium-size onions
2 medium-size white potatoes
1 tablespoon olive oil
1-1/2 cups chicken broth
1-1/2 cups water
1 tablespoon pastina pasta
1 tablespoon grated Parmesan
   cheese

This was my mother's favorite soup to make, and my favorite to eat.

Peel and cut onions and potatoes into 1/2-inch cubes. In a large nonstick pan over medium heat, heat olive oil. Add onions and sauté 5 to 10 minutes, or until translucent. Add potatoes and sauté 3 minutes. Add chicken broth and water. Reduce heat and simmer 15 to 20 minutes, or until vegetables are tender. Add pastina and cook 3 minutes. Pour into soup bowls and sprinkle with Parmesan cheese.

All'Italiana: My mother cooked this soup with onions and potatoes from our garden. It was warm and filling and we all loved to dunk fresh, hot bread into it for a satisfying meal.

Per Serving:
Calories: 181   Total Fat: 5 g   Sat. Fat: 1 g   Chol.: 1 mg

Pea Soup

Zuppa di Piselli

Serves: 4
Preparation Time: 20 minutes
Cooking Time: 25 to 30 minutes

2 medium-size carrots
1 medium-size potato
1 cup green peas (fresh, frozen or canned)
1 quart water
1 chicken bouillon cube
2 tablespoons olive oil
1 medium-size onion, chopped
2 cups water
Salt and pepper to taste
2 tablespoons grated Parmesan cheese (optional)

I think every culture has its own version of pea soup. Here is my favorite—the Italian one, of course.

Peel and cut carrots and potato into 1/4-inch cubes. Set carrots aside. In a large pan over medium heat, cook potato and peas in the 1 quart water and bouillon cube. Cook 5 to 10 minutes, or until vegetables are tender. Remove from heat and let cool. With a slotted spoon, remove peas and potatoes. In a blender set to low speed or a food processor equipped with the metal blade, process peas and potatoes until pureed. Return puree to liquid in pan; set aside. In a medium-size pan over medium heat, heat olive oil. Add onion and sauté 3 to 5 minutes, or until translucent. Add carrots and sauté 1 minute. Add the 2 cups water and simmer 10 to 15 minutes, or until tender. Combine all ingredients in larger pan. Season with salt and pepper. Pour into soup bowls and sprinkle with Parmesan cheese, if desired.

All'Italiana: A nice glass of Barbera or Chianti is the perfect accent to this delicious soup.

Per Serving:
Calories: 188   Total Fat: 8 g   Sat. Fat: 2 g   Chol.: 3 mg

Pesce

Fish & Shellfish

Fish is in. Years ago, clients hardly asked for it except in appetizers, or deep-fried or broiled in butter. Today, fish is taking the place of meat at many of my dinners. More and more clients request it broiled without butter and adorned with fresh vegetables. I have assembled the best of the recipes that are the most popular with my clients. Many I bring from my childhood, such as Baccala Stoccafisso (page 38) and Baccala alla Piancentina (page 39). Some I have learned along the way, such as Salmone e Salsa Verde (page 30). A few were derived from experiments prompted by the desire to create spectacular meals with minimal cholesterol and fat, such as Crostacei al Succo di Arancia (page 32). Fish is delicious, versatile, elegant and a great lowfat and low-cholesterol alternative to red meat and poultry. Enjoy!

Salmon with Green Sauce

Salmone e Salsa Verde

Serves: 4
Preparation Time: 10 minutes
Cooking Time: 20 minutes

1 (1-lb.) salmon fillet
Salt and pepper to taste
2 tablespoons olive oil
1 lemon, thinly sliced

Salsa Verde:
1 (10-oz.) package thawed
  frozen spinach, drained,
  or 1 cup cooked spinach
2 tablespoons olive oil
1 garlic clove, crushed

This is one of the most beautiful dishes I make. It is a must at parties and dinners when it is crucial to make a terrific impression.

Preheat broiler. Prepare Salse Verde; set aside. Season salmon with salt and pepper. Place salmon on a broiler pan. Drizzle olive oil over salmon. Broil 5 to 8 minutes, or until salmon is pale pink with a touch of brown on its surface. When pierced with a fork, salmon should just begin to flake—do not overcook. Place salmon on a serving plate cover w/sauce. To garnish, place lemon slices around salmon.

Salsa Verde
In a food processor equipped with the metal blade, process spinach, olive oil and garlic 15 seconds, or until smooth.

Variation: Salsa Verde can also be served on the side instead on as a garnish.

All'Italiana: This dish is at its best when accompanied by a vegetable dish such as Rosemary Potatoes (page 126).

Per Serving:
Calories: 267   Total Fat: 17 g   Sat. Fat: 2 g   Chol.: 59 mg

Cod with Tomatoes

Merluzzo con Pomodoro

Serves: 4
Preparation Time: 5 minutes
Cooking Time: 20 to 26 minutes

2 pounds cod fillets
2 garlic cloves, chopped
1/2 cup lemon juice
10 basil leaves or 2 tablespoons dried leaf basil
2 pounds fresh tomatoes, chopped, or 32 ounces canned chopped tomatoes

A change from grilled fish, this saucy dish shakes up the image of shy, quiet fish dishes and gives it verve! I made a splash with this at a luncheon hosted by the Junior League in Larchmont, New York.

Spray a large skillet with nonstick cooking spray. Add cod and cook over medium heat 2 to 3 minutes on each side, or until browned. Add garlic and cook 2 to 3 minutes, or until garlic is golden. Stir in lemon juice, basil and tomatoes. Reduce heat, cover and simmer 15 to 20 minutes. When it is done, fish should be opaque and white, not translucent.

All'Italiana: To enjoy this dish at its best, serve with a light polenta dish like Basic Polenta (page 98) or plain rice to absorb the delicious tomato sauce.

Per Serving:
Calories: 200   Total Fat: 2 g   Sat. Fat: 0.4g   Chol.: 128 mg

Scallops in Orange Juice

Crostacei al Succo di Arancia

Serves: 6
Preparation Time: 10 minutes
Cooking Time: 20 minutes

8 ounces orzo pasta
1 tablespoon olive oil
1 cup coarsely chopped celery
1 cup coarsely chopped carrots
1 cup coarsely chopped
   broccoli
1 pound bay scallops
1 cup fresh orange juice
1 pinch of marjoram
1/2 cup slivered almonds
1 tablespoon parsley, coarsely
   chopped
Salt and pepper to taste

On a whim, I cooked fresh bay scallops and vegetables in orange juice instead of just olive oil. My client, Bill Koch, and his family loved it!

Cook pasta according to package directions until al dente. Drain and set aside in a serving bowl. In a wok or large pan over low heat, heat olive oil. Add celery and carrots and cook, covered, 10 minutes. Add broccoli and cook, uncovered, 3 to 5 minutes, stirring frequently. Stir in bay scallops. Toss gently 1 minute and slowly stir in orange juice. Cook over high heat 3 to 5 minutes. Add marjoram, almonds and parsley. Cook 1 minute. Scallops should be tender and opaque. Pour over cooked pasta and toss to combine.

Variations: Use 1 pound jumbo shrimp instead of bay scallops. Shell shrimp, remove veins and cut in half lengthwise. Add to recipe at same time as you would scallops. Shrimp may take longer to cook, so watch carefully. As with scallops, you can serve this over spaghetti, white rice or on its own.

All'Italiana: Italy borrows the best from all cultures—in this case, the Orient. Enjoy this global dish with a chilled glass of Orvieto or Pinot Grigio.

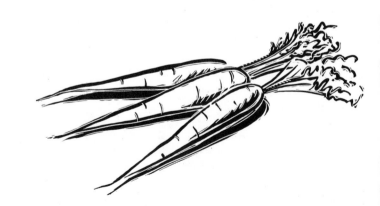

Per Serving:
Calories: 322   Total Fat: 9 g   Sat. Fat: 1 g   Chol.: 25 mg

Scallops in Broth

Crostacei in Brodo

Serves: 4
Preparation Time: 10 minutes
Cooking Time: 30 minutes

2 celery stalks
1 large carrot
1 medium-size onion
1 shallot
1 cup clam juice
1 cup water
1 teaspoon salt
1 teaspoon pepper
1 pound bay or sea scallops
1/2 tablespoon dried leaf Italian
   parsley
1/2 tablespoon dried leaf
   chervil
1/2 tablespoon dried leaf
   tarragon
Cooked white rice (optional)

Adapted from a French recipe, this is an Italian dish that serves the American palate well. When I worked on Long Island, my French wife showed me how to make the most of delicious bay scallops.

Coarsely chop celery, carrot, onion and shallot. In a medium-size pan over medium heat, simmer vegetables in clam juice and water 5 minutes. Add salt and pepper and simmer 20 minutes. Rinse scallops, pat dry and add to broth. Sprinkle with parsley, chervil and tarragon. Simmer 3 to 5 minutes, or until scallops are opaque. Serve over plain white rice or pour into individual bowls as a wonderful first course.

All'Italiana: This is a great prelude to pasta with Genoa Pesto Sauce (page 140) or grilled fish served with plain white rice.

Per Serving:
Calories: 143   Total Fat: 1 g   Sat. Fat: 0.1   Chol.: 37 mg

Mackerel with Fennel in Mustard Sauce

Sqomberi alla Senape e Finocchio

Serves: 6
Preparation Time: 5 minutes
Cooking Time: 12 to 18 minutes

1/2 cup plain nonfat yogurt
1 tablespoon Dijon-style mustard
1 teaspoon white wine vinegar
1 tablespoon olive oil
1 tablespoon fennel seeds
6 mackerel fillets (about 1/4 pound each)
1 lemon, cut into quarters

A succulent dish that's so easy to prepare, it will free you from the kitchen to enjoy your own dinner party.

Preheat oven to 400F (205C). In a large bowl, combine all ingredients, except mackerel and lemon. In a large, shallow baking dish, place mackerel fillets in a single layer. Pour yogurt mixture over mackerel. Bake 12 to 18 minutes until mackerel is opaque and just begins to flake. Before serving, squeeze lemon over fillets.

All'Italiana: A perfect dish for hot summer nights along the Mediterranean. Italians will opt for plain white rice as a perfect backdrop.

Per Serving:
Calories: 262   Total Fat: 18 g   Sat. Fat: 4 g   Chol.: 80 mg

Trout with Porcini Mushrooms

Trota con Funghi

Serves: 2
Preparation Time: 65 minutes including soaking time
Cooking Time: 30 minutes

10 dried porcini mushrooms
1 cup warm water
1/4 cup coarse Italian-flavored dry bread crumbs, crushed
2 trout fillets (about 1/4 pound each)
2 tablespoons olive oil
Salt to taste

An elegant dish with a delicate fragrance and tender texture.

Soak mushrooms in water 1 hour. Preheat oven to 375F (190C). In a large pan over medium heat, simmer mushrooms and water 10 to 15 minutes. Pour mushrooms and water into a baking dish large enough to hold trout in 1 layer. Sprinkle with bread crumbs. Arrange trout fillets in baking dish. Spoon olive oil over trout fillets and sprinkle with salt. Bake 10 minutes. Turn heat to broil and place dish under broiler until the top becomes brown and crisp. Serve in same dish.

All'Italiana: Try this magnificent dish with Risotto alla Vodka (page 104) or Risotto al Forno (page 107) for a completely delicious Italian dinner!

Per Serving:
Calories: 298   Total Fat: 21 g   Sat. Fat: 3 g   Chol.: 65 mg

Roasted Striped Bass

Spigola Arrosto

Serves: 8
Preparation Time: 15 minutes
Cooking Time: 20 minutes
(depending on weight of fish)

1 (4-lb.) whole striped bass, ready for cooking
1 tablespoon all-purpose flour
1 garlic clove
2 teaspoons dried rosemary
1 teaspoon dried leaf oregano
1 teaspoon dried leaf sage
1 teaspoon salt
1 teaspoon pepper
2 tablespoons olive oil

This is an elegant dish which I like to think was served at regal feasts during the Renaissance. I prepare this for very formal parties where a dramatic presentation can turn a dinner into an event.

Preheat oven to 450F (230C). Rinse fish and do not dry. With the heel of your hand, break the spine just below the head. Using a sifter, sprinkle fish with flour. Spray a large nonstick baking pan with nonstick cooking spray. Place fish in baking pan and add garlic. Sprinkle half of rosemary, oregano, sage, salt and pepper inside fish. Then, sprinkle remaining herbs, salt and pepper on top of fish. Pour olive oil over fish. Bake fish on middle rack of oven, 5 minutes per pound. To be sure that fish is done, eyes should be cloudy and flesh should be opaque when pierced with a fork. Remove garlic. To serve, cut fish along side of stomach, lift up meat with a spatula and remove bones. Replace meat and serve.

Variation: Try this with a large fillet of bass. For a 1-pound fillet use 1/4 of ingredients (except garlic which is still 1 clove) and simply sprinkle fillet with herbs instead of tucking them inside fish.

All'Italiana: Serve this delicous and eye-pleasing treat with Rosemary Potatoes (page 126). Although wine is delightful, I sometimes drink a rich beer or ale with this dish.

Per Serving:
Calories: 283   Total Fat: 12 g   Sat. Fat: 2 g   Chol.: 181 mg

Fish in Parchment

Pesce al Cartoccio

Serves: 3 to 4
Preparation Time: 10 minutes
Cooking Time: 5 to 7 minutes

1/4 pound white mushrooms
2 garlic cloves
3/4 cup dry white wine
1 (1-lb.) fish fillet (St. Peter,
   sole, bass, catfish or any
   other boneless fillet).
1 teaspoon dried or fresh
   rosemary leaves
1 tablespoon parsley, coarsely
   chopped

Don't let the name scare you—this elegant dish is a snap to make.

Slice mushrooms thinly, and chop garlic. Preheat oven to 475F (240C). Spray a large nonstick skillet with nonstick cooking spray. Add mushrooms and garlic and cook 2 minutes. Swirl in white wine. Bring to a boil. Remove from heat. Cut parchment paper or foil into a 15-inch-long strip. Spoon 1 tablespoon of liquid from pan onto paper. Lay the fish fillet on top. With a slotted spoon, remove mushrooms and garlic from pan and place on fillet. Spoon 2 more tablespoons of liquid on top. Sprinkle with rosemary and parsley. Fold paper neatly around the fish, making sure closing is secure. Bake 5 to 7 minutes. To test for doneness, open paper carefully and pierce fish with a fork. The fish should be opaque and just beginning to flake.

Variations: Use 12 dried porcini mushrooms soaked in 2 cups warm water 1 hour instead of fresh mushrooms. Foil works just as well as parchment paper, but the paper will make a more impressive presentation.

All'Italiana: A perfect side dish for this fish is Rosemary Potatoes (page 126).

Per Serving:
Calories: 257   Total Fat: 2 g   Sat. Fat: 5 g   Chol.: 56 mg

Cod Fish Pâté

Baccala Stoccafisso

Serves: 10
Preparation Time: 15 minutes plus 2 days soaking time
Cooking Time: 5 to 7 minutes

2 pounds dried salt cod
1 cup olive oil
1/2 cup parsley, finely chopped
1 garlic clove, minced
1/2 teaspoon salt
1/2 teaspoon pepper
1 pinch of nutmeg
2 or 3 parsley sprigs

This classic peasant dish is a throwback to the ages before refrigeration when fish had to be salted and dried in order to keep.

Two days before you wish to serve this dish, soak salt cod in enough water to cover completely. Be sure to change water 2 to 4 times and to let cod soak in a cool place. If you are using presoaked cod, additional soaking is not necessary. In a large pan over medium heat, cook cod in enough water to cover. Bring to a boil. Reduce heat and cook 5 minutes. With a spatula, remove fish from pan and place on a cutting board. With a fork, flake fish, and with your fingers, remove any bones. Spread fish out onto surface to cool. When cod is cool, in a food processor equipped with the metal blade, or a mortar, process cod until it becomes a paste. Transfer cod paste into a large bowl. Stir with a spoon, adding olive oil very slowly. Continue stirring until cod paste turns very white. Add chopped parsley, garlic, salt, pepper and nutmeg. Transfer cod paste to a fish mold or shape with a spatula into a serving dish. If using a fish mold, refrigerate for 10 minutes and then turn it out onto a serving dish. If just using a serving dish, you can serve cod immediately. Garnish with parsley.

All'Italiana: Once exclusively a peasant dish served with bread and slices of tomatoes as a meal, Baccula Stoccafisso is now a popular choice at Italian buffets.

Per Serving:
Calories: 453   Total Fat: 24 g   Sat. Fat: 3 g   Chol.: 138 mg

Dried Salted Cod, Piancentina Style

Baccala alla Piancentina

Serves: 4
Preparation Time: 5 minutes
plus 1 day soaking time
Cooking Time: 30 minutes

1 (1-lb.) dried salt cod fillet
2 tablespoons all-purpose flour
2 tablespoons olive oil
4 garlic cloves, minced
2 tablespoons tomato paste
1/2 cup water
1 tablespoon parsley, coarsely
    chopped

In southern Italian slang, baccala means money—a fitting nickname for this fish so rich in flavor!

If starting from scratch, soak cod fillet in 1 quart of water 24 hours. For best results, replace water 2 or 3 times. When ready to prepare, pat cod fillet dry and dust with flour. In a large nonstick skillet over high heat, heat olive oil. Add cod and cook 2 minutes. Turn cod fillet over. Cook 1 minute. Add garlic. Cook 1 minute. Stir in tomato paste and water to make a sauce. Reduce heat and cover. Simmer 20 to 25 minutes. Arrange on a platter and sprinkle with parsley.

Variation: Presoaked salt cod can be found at most butchers, gourmet shops and supermarkets.

All'Italiana: When I was a boy, we ate dried salt cod in place of more expensive red meats and fresh fish. What I once thought to be poor man's dish, I now regard as a meal fit for a king.

Per Serving:
Calories: 410   Total Fat: 10 g   Sat. Fat: 2g   Chol.: 172 mg

Seafood Lasagna

Lasagne di Pescatore

Serves: 6
Preparation Time: 15 minutes
Cooking Time: 30 minutes

10 lasagna noodles
2 cups chopped broccoli
2 cups chopped tomatoes
   (fresh or canned)
3/4 cup plus 1 tablespoon
   coarse plain bread crumbs,
   crushed
3 very thin fillets of sole,
   flounder or red snapper
1 tablespoon dried leaf basil or
   1/4 cup chopped fresh basil
1 tablespoon dried leaf
   marjoram
1/4 teaspoon salt
1/4 teaspoon pepper
1 tablespoon olive oil

The classic Italian dish gets a makeover.

Cook the lasagne noodles according to package directions until al dente. Drain. Preheat oven to 400F (205C). In a medium-size bowl, mix broccoli, tomatoes and 3/4 cup of the bread crumbs. Spray an 11" X 8" lasagne dish with nonstick cooking spray. Line the bottom with broccoli mixture about 1/2 inch deep. Add a single layer of lasagne noodles. Cut fish fillets in 1-inch-long strips and lay on top of noodles, leaving an inch between each fish strip. In between each fish strip, add some more broccoli mixture. Sprinkle with herbs, salt, pepper and olive oil. Arrange remaining lasagne strips and broccoli mixture on top. Sprinkle the 1 tablespoon bread crumbs on top. Bake 15 to 20 minutes, or until fish and vegetables are cooked.

Variation: Two cups fresh spinach can be used instead of broccoli.

All'Italiana: Savor this dish

with an Orvieto or Pinot

Grigio wine.

Per Serving:
Calories: 289   *Total Fat: 4 g*   *Sat. Fat: 0.5 g*   *Chol.: 18 mg*

Pollame e Uove

Poultry & Eggs

Here are recipes focusing on an ingredient that enjoys superstar acclaim as well as one that has fallen to almost criminal status: poultry and eggs.

Chicken is dressed in tarragon and rosemary, covered in succulent tomato sauces, surrounded with squash or baked in whisky and smothered in vermouth. Turkey is juicy when cooked with fresh vegetables and takes the place of pork and beef in classic meatballs and burgers.

Eggs shouldn't be off-limits to people concerned about cholesterol when only egg whites or egg substitutes are used. In the following recipes, they are combined with tomatoes, peppers, spinach, anchovies and other Italian flavors to make them spectacular and nutritious for everyone to enjoy.

Tarragon Chicken

Pollo al Dragoncello

Serves: 4
Preparation Time: 5 minutes
Cooking Time: 30 minutes

1 (3- to 4-lb.) roasting chicken
1 teaspoon salt
1 teaspoon pepper
1 tablespoon dried leaf
    tarragon
1/2 cup water

When roasting a whole chicken, I prefer to cook the chicken with the skin and let my guests remove it themselves. I find that removing the skin before roasting frequently results in dry chicken.

Preheat oven to 375F (190C). Rub chicken with salt and pepper. Make tiny cuts into chicken and slip half of tarragon inside cuts and sprinkle the rest over top of chicken. Place chicken in a roasting pan and cook 30 minutes, basting every 15 minutes. Add water to the pan. Turn chicken upside down and cook 30 minutes, basting every 15 minutes, or until juice runs clear when a thigh is pierced with a fork or knife. Remove skin and carve before serving, or leave it to your guests to remove skin if desired.

Variation: Use about 1/4 cup loosely packed fresh tarragon instead of dried tarragon. French chefs add 1/4 cup fresh truffles in addition to tarragon.

All'Italiana: A great family dinner, especially when served outdoors in the summer.

Per Serving:
Calories: 325   Total Fat: 13 g   Sat. Fat: 10 g   Chol.: 152 mg

Chicken with Butternut Squash

Petti di Pollo con Zucca

Serves: 6
Preparation Time: 20 minutes
Cooking Time: 35 to 40 minutes

6 boneless chicken breasts
1/2 cup all-purpose flour
1 medium-size butternut
   squash, cut into 1-inch cubes
1/2 tablespoon dried leaf
   tarragon
2 tablespoons honey
2 tablespoons dry vermouth
Salt
Pepper
1/2 tablespoon paprika
   (optional)

I used to prepare this dish for Joan Fontaine in the 1970s. Always ahead of her time, she asked me to remove the skin from the chicken. She knew back then to limit the fat and cholesterol in her diet.

Preheat oven to 375F (190C). Remove skin and excess fat from chicken breasts. Pour flour onto a plate. Roll chicken breasts in flour until well coated. Spray a large nonstick skillet with nonstick cooking spray. Add chicken breasts and cook over medium heat 5 to 7 minutes, or until both sides are golden-brown. Set aside. In a steamer or medium-size pan filled with enough water to cover squash, steam squash 6 minutes or boil 3 to 5 minutes, or until tender. Place chicken breasts in a nonstick baking dish. Arrange butternut squash around chicken breasts. In a small bowl, combine tarragon, honey and vermouth. Brush mixture onto chicken breasts. Sprinkle chicken with salt, pepper and paprika, if using. Bake 20 to 30 minutes, basting with pan juices every 5 minutes. Chicken is done when juices run clear when pierced with a fork.

Variation: Use about 2 tablespoons fresh tarragon in plce of dried tarragon

All'Italiana: Drink a good Orvieto or Pinot Grigio wine with this luscious dish.

Per Serving:
Calories: 284   Total Fat: 6 g   Sat. Fat: 0.2g   Chol.: 146 mg

Hunter's Chicken

Pollo alla Cacciatore

Serves: 4
Preparation Time: 10 minutes
plus overnight soaking time
Cooking Time: 30 minutes

10 dried porcini mushrooms
1 cup water
4 chicken thighs
2 garlic cloves, minced
2 cups chopped Roma
   tomatoes (canned or fresh)
3 tablespoons tomato paste
12 pitted ripe olives, coarsely
   chopped
1 tablespoon parsley, finely
   chopped

Historically, this dish has done wonders for weary hunters back from battling nature's elements.

Soak mushrooms in water overnight. When ready to cook, pull off skin from chicken and remove excess fat. Spray a large nonstick skillet with nonstick cooking spray. Add chicken and cook over medium heat 6 minutes, until browned on all sides. Add garlic, tomatoes, tomato paste and mushrooms. Reduce heat, cover and simmer 20 minutes, or until chicken is tender. Add olives and parsley. Cover and simmer 5 minutes, or until chicken is tender.

All'Italiana: Serve this

delectable dish with plain

fettucini. The sauce will coat

the fettucini to make a

heavenly dining experience.

Per Serving:
Calories: 161   Total Fat: 8 g   Sat. Fat: 2 g   Chol.: 49 mg

Chicken Roasted with Lean Bacon

Pollo con Lardo Affumicato

Serves: 4 to 8
Preparation Time: 10 minutes
Cooking Time: 25 to 30 minutes

8 boneless chicken breast halves
1 teaspoon salt
1 teaspoon pepper
1/3 tablespoon dried leaf marjoram
1/3 tablespoon dried leaf oregano
1/3 tablespoon dried rosemary
24 strips bacon substitute or lean bacon

Lean bacon will make chicken juicy and succulent.

Preheat oven to 425F (220C). Remove skin and excess fat from chicken. Place chicken between 2 layers of waxed paper. Pound chicken with kitchen mallet 3 or 4 times on each side. Remove from waxed paper. With your hands, rub salt, pepper and herbs onto chicken. Roll each chicken breast widthwise and wrap with 3 strips of lean bacon.into tidy packages. Place chicken on top of a rack in a roasting pan so that fat can run off and away from chicken. Cook 25 to 30 minutes, turning chicken over every 10 minutes, or until juices run clear when chicken is pierced with a fork.

All'Italiana: Wild rice or a sweet squash puree will complement this terrific dish in a fine Italian way.

Per Serving:
Calories: 292   Total Fat: 18 g   Sat. Fat: 3g   Chol.: 176 mg

Three-Day Chicken

Pollo per Tre Giorni

Serves: 2 to 4
Preparation Time: 20 minutes
to prepare chicken, plus time
to prepare individual recipes
Cooking Time: Varies, 2 to 3
hours for broth

1 (3- to 4-lb.) roasting chicken

Chicken Broth:
1 carrot
1 onion
Water

Don't let the name scare you. You don't cook the chicken for three days—you can enjoy three days' worth of meals from one chicken.

Rinse chicken inside and out. Cut chicken down center of breast. With a sharp paring knife, cut breast away from bones. Separate legs from chicken and save giblets. Wrap legs and refrigerate for use the next day. Store carcass, wings and giblets in an airtight container and refrigerate. Prepare chicken breasts any way you like. The next day, prepare Hunter's Chicken (page 46), using chicken legs. On the third day, add bones, wings, giblets, carrot and onion and enough water to cover to a large pot. Boil 5 minutes, then let simmer 2 to 3 hours and use chicken broth in favorite recipe for soup.

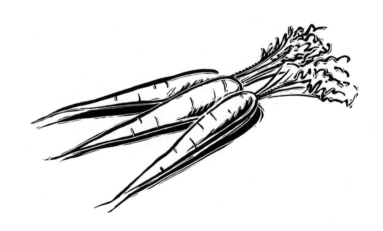

All'Italiana: I made a practice of cooking chicken like this when I was struggling on my own in Paris.

Chicken Breasts with Vermouth

Petti di Pollo al Vermouth

Serves: 2
Preparation Time: 10 minutes
Cooking Time: 15 to 20 minutes

2 boneless chicken breasts
1 tablespoon all-purpose flour
1 pinch of salt
1 pinch of pepper
1 tablespoon margarine
1 cup dry white vermouth

The quintessential Italian aperitif adds its distinct flavor to chicken. This is an incredibly delicious switch from chicken sautéed with white wine.

Preheat oven to 275F (135C). Remove skin and excess fat from chicken and discard. Place chicken between 2 layers of waxed paper. Pound chicken with kitchen mallet 5 times on each side. In a flat dish, combine flour, salt and pepper. Remove waxed paper from chicken. Roll chicken in flour mixture until well coated. In a large nonstick skillet over medium heat, melt margarine. Add chicken and cook 3 to 5 minutes on each side, or until golden and meat is white all the way through. Remove chicken from pan and keep warm on an ovenproof serving plate in oven. To the same pan over medium heat, add vermouth. Stir well, scraping the bottom of the pan lightly so that margarine and chicken particles on the bottom of the pan will mix in with vermouth. Cook 5 to 10 minutes, or until vermouth is reduced to about 2 tablespoons. Pour over chicken and serve.

All'Italiana: Simplicity is beautiful. Serve this with white rice and you'll have a flavorful, authentic Italian meal.

Per Serving:
Calories: 368   Total Fat: 12 g   Sat. Fat: 18 g   Chol.: 146 mg

Drunk Chicken

Pollo al Whisky

Serves: 4
Preparation Time: 15 minutes
Cooking Time: 50 to 60 minutes

1 (2-lb.) broiler-fryer chicken, cut into serving pieces
1/2 cup Scotch whisky
2 tablespoons margarine
1/2 cup thinly sliced white mushrooms
Juice from half a lemon
1 shallot, minced
1/2 cup plain nonfat yogurt
1/2 teaspoon salt
1/2 teaspoon pepper
1/2 teaspoon cornstarch mixed with 1/2 cup plain nonfat yogurt
1 teaspoon lemon juice

Leave it to the Italians to find a way to eat whisky. Delizioso!

Rinse chicken and remove skin. Spray a large skillet with nonstick cooking spray. Add chicken and cook over medium heat 10 minutes, turning once, or until golden-brown on both sides. Add whisky. Reduce heat and cover. Cook 10 minutes. In a small pan over medium heat, melt margarine. Add mushrooms and cook 2 minutes. Add juice from lemon half to mushrooms and cook 3 to 5 minutes, or until moisture disappears. Add to cooking chicken. Stir in shallot, the 1/2 cup yogurt, salt and pepper. Cover and simmer 20 to 25 minutes. Do not boil. Remove chicken, place on a platter and keep warm. Increase heat under skillet and stir cornstarch mixture into sauce. Cook, stirring, until combined and sauce comes to a simmer. Add the 1 teaspoon lemon juice. Pour over chicken and serve.

All'Italiana: Again, Italians find a way to use a product from another culture and make it uniquely theirs. It works best served with plain rice.

Per Serving:
Calories: 410   Total Fat: 13 g   Sat. Fat: 3 g   Chol.: 90 mg

Roasted Chicken, Italian Style

Pollo Arrosto All'Italiana

Serves: 6
Preparation Time: 10 minutes
Cooking Time: 1 hour

1 (3- to 4-lb.) roasting chicken
    with giblets
1 tablespoon dried rosemary
1 tablespoon plus a pinch dried
    leaf sage
1 teaspoon salt
1/2 tablespoon dried leaf thyme
2 cups water
3 tablespoons white wine

A simple dish that will make your mouth water. I suggest leaving on the skin while cooking and removing it later to ensure a juicy, tender chicken.

Preheat oven to 375F (190C). Remove giblets from chicken, rinse them and set aside. Rinse chicken. Break breast bone with heel of your hand. Place chicken in a shallow baking pan. Loosen an area of skin next to the breast bone about 5 or 6 inches long and 2 inches wide. Tuck half of the rosemary and the 1 tablespoon sage under skin. Slip a pinch of sage inside cavity of chicken. Sprinkle with salt, remaining rosemary and the thyme. In a medium-size saucepan over medium heat, cook giblets, except liver, in water. Add more water, 1/2 cup at a time, to giblets as water evaporates and is used. Place chicken in oven and cook 30 minutes, basting every 15 minutes with broth from giblets simmering on stove. Add white wine to baking pan. Cook 30 minutes longer, or until juices run clear when chicken is pierced with a fork. Place chicken on a platter and spoon juice from bottom of pan over chicken. Discard giblets. Carve chicken in the kitchen or at the table.

All'Italiana: The best white wine to use in this dish is the same wine you will be serving at dinner, preferably an Orvieto or Pinot Grigio.

Per Serving:
Calories: 216   Total Fat: 9 g   Sat. Fat: 3 g   Chol.: 102 mg

Italian Chicken Fingers

Giulienne di Pollo

Serves: 4
Preparation Time: 20 minutes
Cooking Time: 5 minutes

1/2 head red leaf lettuce
1/2 bunch arugala
2 heads Belgian endive
3 ounces feta cheese
1 pound boneless chicken
   breasts
1 teaspoon garlic powder
1 teaspoon dried parsley
Pinch of salt
Pinch of pepper
1/2 cup sliced blanched
   almonds

Italian Salad Dressing:
3 tablespoons olive oil
2 tablespoons red wine vinegar
Pinch of salt
Pinch of pepper

Believe it or not, Americans have not cornered the market on chicken fingers. They are found at many Italian dinner parties, too! I first made this at a dinner prepared for Joshua Logan, the film director.

Rinse and dry red leaf lettuce and arugala and cut off ends and stems. Rinse and dry Belgian endive. Tear lettuce and arugala into bite-size pieces and shred endive. Place a handful of each onto 4 dinner plates. Cut cheese into bite-size cubes and arrange over salad greens. Refrigerate or set aside in a cool place. Remove skin and cut off excess fat from chicken breasts. Cut breasts lengthwise into 1/2-inch strips. Combine garlic powder, parsley, salt and pepper on a plate and roll chicken strips into mixture until coated. Spray a large skillet with nonstick cooking spray. Add chicken strips and almond slices and cook over medium heat 4 to 5 minutes, or until chicken is white all the way through. Prepare dressing. Divide chicken and almonds among plates and drizzle with dressing.

Italian Salad Dressing
In a small bowl, whisk all ingredients together.

Variations: Feel free to substitute your favorite salad greens for the ones listed here. Also, Romano cheese can be substituted for feta.

All'Italiana: Enjoy this meal as a light lunch or dinner *al fresco* with a glass of Merlot or Orvieto.

Per Serving:
Calories: 200   Total Fat: 7 g   Sat. Fat: 2 g   Chol.: 32 mg

Julia's Special Turkey

Tacchino alla Giulia

Serves: 8 to 10
Preparation Time: 20 minutes plus 1 hour cooling time
Cooking Time: 70 minutes

Breast of Turkey (page 55)
1 small onion, chopped
1/2 cup white wine
Pinch of salt

Potato Topping:
3 medium-size russet potatoes
1 tablespoon margarine
About 2 tablespoons skim milk
2 tablespoons grated Parmesan cheese

This was one of my mother's specialties and I love it to this day. It was her version of a shepherd's pie.

Prepare Breast of Turkey (page 55). While turkey is cooling, prepare topping. Set aside. Remove bone from turkey breast and discard. Cut turkey into chunks. In a food processor equipped with the metal blade, process turkey, vegetables and garlic from pot 10 to 20 seconds, or until finely chopped. In a medium-size pan over medium heat, cook onion with white wine and salt 5 minutes, or until translucent. Preheat broiler. In a large bowl, combine turkey mixture and onion mixture. Pour combined mixture into an ungreased baking dish. Spoon mashed potatoes on top. Sprinkle with Parmesan cheese. Broil 10 to 15 minutes, or until top is golden-brown.

Potato Topping

Cut unpeeled potatoes into 1-inch rounds. Cook potatoes in boiling water in a medium-size pan over medium heat until tender. Drain and peel. Return potatoes to pan over medium heat and add margarine. With a fork or whisk, mash potatoes. Stir in milk until potatoes are soft and fluffy but not soupy. Set aside.

Variation: Packaged mashed potatoes work just as well as homemade. Just follow the package instructions and use the same way you would the fresh.

All'Italiana: This dish will always remind me of my childhood. My mother would substitute chicken, beef, or pork for turkey.

Per Serving:
Calories: 260   Total Fat: 9 g   Sat. Fat: 2 g   Chol.: 83 mg

Turkey Meatballs

Polpette di Tacchino

Serves: 4
Preparation Time: 20 minutes
Cooking Time: 30 to 35 minutes

1 pound ground turkey
3/4 cup coarse Italian-seasoned bread crumbs, crushed
1 medium-size onion, grated
2 egg whites
1/2 teaspoon dried leaf marjoram
1/2 teaspoon dried leaf oregano
1/4 teaspoon salt
1/4 teaspoon pepper
1/2 cup white wine, beer or water
2 cups Classic Tomato Sauce (page 141) or purchased tomato pasta sauce

Instead of beef or pork meatballs try this on pasta, rice or polenta—you'll never go back!

Preheat broiler. In a large bowl, combine turkey, bread crumbs, grated onion, egg whites, marjoram, oregano, salt and pepper. This is best mixed with your hands. Slowly pour wine into turkey mixture. Mix with your hands 1 minute or until mixture forms a large ball. Shape into small uniform meatballs and place in a shallow ungreased non-stick baking pan. Place dish under broiler until meatballs are browned. When they are done, set oven to 350F (175C). Remove pan with meatballs. Cover meatballs with tomato sauce. Bake 30 to 35 minutes, or until meatballs are firm and no longer pink in center and sauce is bubbly. Spoon meatballs and sauce over cooked pasta, rice or polenta and serve.

Variation: Instead of egg whites, use 1/2 cup egg substitute.

All'Italiana: Tear off a piece of Italian bread and soak up the leftover sauce on your plate. You're at home, so indulge Italian style!

Per Serving (without pasta or rice):
Calories: 434   Total Fat: 29 g   Sat. Fat: 6 g   Chol.: 165 mg

Breast of Turkey

Filetto di Tacchino

Serves: 6 to 8
Preparation Time: 25 minutes plus 1 hour cooling time
Cooking Time: 70 minutes

1 (2- to 3-lb.) half turkey breast with bone
About 2 cups chicken broth
2 cups water
2 medium-size carrots, thinly sliced
1 medium-size onion, thinly sliced
2 celery stalks, chopped
1 garlic clove, minced

Great as a main course, but spectacular cold in a sandwich.

Remove skin from turkey breast. Fit turkey breast into a small, deep pan. (This recipe works best if it is a tight fit). In a large pan over medium heat, bring 2 cups chicken broth, water, carrots, onion, celery and garlic to a boil. Reduce heat and simmer 3 to 5 minutes until vegetables are tender. Pour over turkey breast. Chicken broth mixture should come up about 1-1/2 inches above the turkey breast. If it doesn't, add more chicken broth as needed. Place pan over high heat and bring liquid to a boil. Reduce heat and cover. Simmer 45 to 50 minutes. Remove from heat and let cool 1 hour at room temperature. Remove bone from turkey breast and discard. Slice cooled turkey breast for sandwiches or a cold cut plate or wrap turkey breast in plastic wrap and refrigerate up to 2 days for later use. Reserve broth and vegetables in an airtight container and freeze for use in soups. When ready for a sandwich or cold cut plate, remove turkey breast from refrigerator and slice if refrigerated whole.

Variation: If you wish, serve this recipe hot in a traditional manner. Cut it into 4 individual servings and smother with cooked vegetables from pot.

All'Italiana: Be very Italian and serve slices of this delicious turkey cold, or heated with one of the many delicious sauces in the Sauces & Garnishes chapter.

Per Serving:
Calories: 188   Total Fat: 4 g   Sat. Fat: 1 g   Chol.: 70 mg

Tuna Talks Turkey

Tacchino Tonnato

Serves: 6 to 8
Preparation Time: 20 minutes
Cooking Time: 1 hour

Breast of Turkey (page 55)
1 tablespoon capers
1 lemon, thinly sliced

Tuna Sauce:

1 (6-1/8-oz.) can white
    albacore tuna packed in oil
3/4 cup Tofunetta (page 132)
10 to 15 anchovy fillets
Juice from 1 lemon

Wake up dozing tastebuds, we've got a surprise for you! The daring duo of turkey and tuna in the same dish add up to an experience that will send you into orbit!

Prepare Breast of Turkey (page 55). Remove from heat and let cool 1 hour. Remove turkey breast from pan and discard bone. Place turkey on a platter. Save broth and vegetables in an airtight container and freeze for future use in soups or other recipes. Prepare sauce. Pour sauce over cold turkey breast on platter. Garnish with capers and lemon slices.

Tuna Sauce

Drain oil from tuna. In a blender set at high speed or a food processor equipped with the metal blade, process tuna, Tofunetta, anchovy fillets and lemon juice 10 seconds.

All'Italiana: Dining outdoors is the most beautiful way to savor this dish. I always serve it with a dark green leafy salad to make a cool dinner on a hot summer night.

Per Serving:
Calories: 310   Total Fat: 10 g   Sat. Fat: 2 g   Chol.: 81 mg

Turkey Burgers

Tacchino all'Americana

Serves: 4
Preparation Time: 15 minutes
Cooking Time: 12 to 15 minutes

1/2 pound ground turkey
1/4 cup liquid egg substitute
3/4 cup coarse Italian-flavored bread crumbs
1 tablespoon sunflower oil
1 cup thinly sliced white mushrooms
1/2 cup chicken broth
1/2 cup Tofunetta (see page 132)

Italians caught the craving for burgers years ago. But like everything else they've made them their own with a distinctively Italian flair. Turkey burgers are no exception.

Preheat oven to 275F (135C). With your hands combine turkey with egg substitute. Separate mixture into 4 or 5 balls, then flatten into patties (burgers). Pour bread crumbs onto a plate. Coat turkey burgers with bread crumbs. Spray a large nonstick skillet with nonstick cooking spray. Add turkey burgers and cook over medium heat 3 to 5 minutes on each side, or until each side is golden-brown and the center no longer pink. Remove from heat. Transfer turkey burgers to a shallow baking dish and place in oven to keep warm. In the same pan, heat sunflower oil. Add mushrooms and sauté 5 minutes, or until softened. Stir chicken broth and Tofunetta into pan and bring liquid to a boil. Remove turkey from oven and place on individual dinner plates or a serving platter. Serve turkey burgers with sauce.

Variations: Whole-wheat bread crumbs can be used instead of Italian-flavored bread crumbs. Also, 1/2 cup plain nonfat yogurt can be used instead of Tofunetta, and 2 egg whites can be used instead of liquid egg substitute.

All'Italiana: Serve turkey burgers on a bed of orzo pasta or white rice and garnish with roasted Italian peppers.

Per Serving:
Calories: 219   Total Fat: 11 g   Sat. Fat: 2 g   Chol.: 44 mg

Baked Egg Whites in Tomato Shells

Uove al Pomodoro in Forno

Serves: 4
Preparation Time: 20 minutes
Cooking Time: 7 minutes

4 very ripe, large red tomatoes
8 egg whites
8 anchovy fillets, or to taste
1 tablespoon capers
1/4 teaspoon salt
1/4 teaspoon black pepper
1/4 teaspoon hot red pepper
  flakes
1 tablespoon grated Romano
  cheese (optional)

Delicious and so easy to make, these are perfect for lunch.

Preheat oven to 400F (205C). Cut off stem ends of tomatoes. Scoop out seeds using a spoon. Place each tomato in its own round baking dish or in a muffin cup. Pour 2 egg whites into each tomato. Crisscross 2 (or more) anchovy fillets across each tomato and sprinkle each with a few capers. Sprinkle with salt, black pepper and pepper flakes. Sprinkle with Romano cheese, if desired. Bake 7 minutes, or until egg whites are set.

Variation: Use 1 cup liquid egg substitute instead of egg whites.

All'Italiana: If you are enjoying this at a relaxed gathering, serve hearty Italian bread with this dish and dunk away in the tomato juices. *Delizioso!*

Per Serving:
Calories: 77   Total Fat: 1 g   Sat. Fat: 0.2g   Chol.: 7 mg

Eggs Stuffed with Red Pepper

Uove Farcite con Peperone

Serves: 6
Preparation Time: 15 minutes
Cooking Time: 20 minutes

6 eggs
1 quart water
1 red bell pepper, quartered
1 tablespoon olive oil
1 tablespoon lemon juice
1/4 teaspoon salt
1/4 teaspoon black pepper
3 large pitted ripe olives, sliced
    into 3 or 4 rounds
12 anchovy fillets

This dish is gorgeous. I hear raves whenever I serve it!

In a medium-size pan, bring eggs and water to a boil. Reduce heat and let eggs simmer 11 minutes. Drain and cool with cold water. Carefully remove shells. Set eggs aside. In a blender set to high speed or a food processor equipped with the metal blade, process bell pepper 10 seconds. Transfer bell pepper to a medium-size bowl and stir in olive oil, lemon juice, salt and black pepper. Slice eggs in half. Remove egg yolks and discard. Spoon red bell pepper mixture into egg halves. Garnish with sliced olives and anchovies.

All'Italiana: Serve this as a unique treat at a brunch or lunch buffet.

Per Serving:
Calories: 60   *Total Fat: 3 g*   *Sat. Fat: 0.5 g*   *Chol.: 7 mg*

Eggs with Tangy Filling

Uove Farcite Mantovane

Serves: 6
Preparation Time: 15 minutes
Cooking Time: About 15 minutes

6 eggs
1 quart water
1/4 cup liquid egg substitute
1 tablespoon Dijon-style mustard
1/2 teaspoon Worcestershire sauce
Salt and pepper to taste
3 large pitted ripe olives, sliced into 3 or 4 rounds
12 anchovy fillets

Straight from the Inferno. Deviled eggs—Italian style!

In a medium-size pan, bring eggs and water to a boil. Reduce heat and simmer eggs 11 minutes. Drain and cool with cold water. Carefully remove shells. Set eggs aside. Spray a medium-size nonstick skillet with nonstick cooking spray. Add liquid egg substitute and cook over medium heat, stirring, 3 to 4 minutes. Set aside. Cut hardcooked eggs in half and remove and discard yolks. In a medium-size bowl, combine scrambled egg substitute, mustard, Worcestershire sauce, salt and pepper. Fill egg halves with egg mixture. Garnish with sliced olives and anchovies.

All'Italiana: The anchovy fillets make this dish stand out as *molto Italiano!*

Per Serving:
Calories: 46   Total Fat: 2 g   Sat. Fat: 0.3 g   Chol.: 7 mg

Eggs Prepared with Leeks

Uove e Porri

Serves: 4
Preparation Time: 20 minutes
Cooking Time: 25 to 30 minutes

10 eggs
2 quarts water
5 or 6 medium-size leeks
7 tablespoons margarine
1/4 cup all-purpose flour
3 cups skim milk
1/2 cup Classic Tomato Sauce
    (page 141) or purchased
    tomato pasta sauce
1/2 cup shredded reduced-
    cholesterol Cheddar cheese

This is an exotic way to serve eggs sure to beat scrambled eggs for presentation appeal every time.

In a large pan, bring eggs and water to a boil. Reduce heat and simmer eggs 11 minutes. Drain and cool with cold water. Carefully remove shells. Cut eggs in half and discard yolks. Slice hard-boiled egg whites crosswise into thin slices and set aside. Cut off and discard green tops from leeks. Make a cut down each leek, cutting each almost halfway through. Rinse under running water to remove sand. Cut leeks into 3/4-inch pieces. Rinse well in a colander. In a medium-size nonstick pan over medium heat, melt 2 tablespoons of the margarine. Add leeks and cook 5 to 10 minutes, or until tender. Add a little water if leeks begin to stick. Set aside. In a medium-size nonstick pan over medium heat, combine 5 tablespoons of the margarine and flour. Whisk until smooth, adding a tablespoon more flour at a time if too sticky. Stir in skim milk until thickened and very smooth. Remove from heat. Preheat broiler. Transfer leeks into a shallow baking pan. Cover with white sauce. Top with hard-cooked egg white slices. Cover with half of the tomato sauce. Sprinkle with Cheddar cheese. Pour remaining tomato sauce around the edges, as if it were framing cheese. Broil 10 minutes, or until top is brown. Serve very hot.

All'Italiana: My mother made a much simpler version of this dish. She did without the creamy sauce and simply combined leeks, eggs, tomato sauce and Parmesan cheese.

Per Serving:
Calories: 452   Total Fat: 23 g   Sat. Fat: 5 g   Chol.: 13 mg

Classic Florentine-Style Baked Eggs

Uove Sformate Fiorentine

Serves: 6
Preparation Time: 20 minutes
Cooking Time: 40 minutes

6 eggs
1 quart water
1 tablespoon margarine
1 tablespoon olive oil
1 small red onion, chopped
2 (10-oz.) packages frozen
   spinach
1/2 teaspoon salt
3 tablespoons margarine
3 tablespoons all-purpose flour
1 cup skim milk
1/2 cup plus 1 tablespoon
   grated Parmesan cheese
1 pinch of nutmeg
1/4 pound reduced-fat and
   cholesterol boiled ham, cut
   in thin strips

The beautiful city of Florence has an incredible local cuisine and one of its features stands out as quintessentially Florentine—spinach! Here the vegetable is used to add pizzazz to baked eggs.

In a large pan, bring eggs and water to a boil. Reduce heat and simmer eggs 11 minutes. Drain and cool with cold water. Carefully remove shells. Cut eggs in half and discard yolks. Chop egg whites and set aside in a small bowl. In a large nonstick pan over medium heat, melt 1 tablespoon margarine with olive oil. Add red onion, cover and cook, stirring occasionally, 5 to 10 minutes, or until translucent. Add frozen spinach and salt. Cover and cook 10 to 12 minutes, or until all liquid disappears. Remove from heat and set aside. In a medium-size nonstick pan over medium heat, combine margarine and flour. Whisk 3 to 5 minutes, or until smooth. Slowly, stir in skim milk. Stir well 2 to 3 minutes, or until thickened and smooth. Add the 1 tablespoon Parmesan cheese and nutmeg and cook 2 minutes. Preheat broiler. Transfer spinach mixture into a shallow baking pan. Sprinkle with egg whites. Place strips of ham over egg whites. Pour sauce over dish. Sprinkle with remaining Parmesan cheese. Broil 10 minutes.

Variations: Use 2-1/2 cups fresh spinach instead of frozen spinach. Instead of ham, smoked turkey can be used.

All'Italiana: Instead of eggs Benedict, Italians indulge in this less-fatty and more delicious egg dish.

Per Serving:
Calories: 242   Total Fat: 14 g   Sat. Fat: 4 g   Chol.: 18 mg

Carne

Beef, Lamb, Pork & Veal

These great tasting meats don't have to be off-limits to people watching their fat and cholesterol intake. Of course, we shouldn't eat red meat every night, nor should we eat it fried in butter or covered in creamy sauces like we used to—but the recipes listed here will let you prepare beef, lamb, pork and veal with the least cholesterol and fat possible. The recipes are wonderful and they're the only way I'll prepare these meats now. See, you can have your meat and eat it too!

Another bit of great news is that there is an alternative to veal raised in the traditional manner. Many people have given up eating veal, but now everyone can enjoy their Italian veal favorites. Ask your butcher about range-fed veal.

Leg of Lamb

Stracotto di Agnello

Serves: 10
Preparation Time: 20 minutes
Cooking Time: 4-1/2 hours

1 (5-lb.) leg of lamb
3 garlic cloves
2 tablespoons olive oil
1 teaspoon salt
1 teaspoon pepper
1 cup baby carrots
6 medium-size onions,
    quartered
2 cups dry white wine
1 cup beef broth
2 bay leaves
2 very ripe tomatoes, chopped
1 cup Classic Tomato Sauce
    (page 141) or purchased
    tomato pasta sauce
1 pinch of pepper
1 pinch of salt
1 cup water

All'Italiana: Served cold, this lamb dish makes a terrific sandwich. Prepare it with dark leafy lettuce, red ripe tomatoes and perhaps some Genoa Pesto Sauce (page 140).

The aroma of garlic and the sweet flavor of vegetables makes this lamb dish a knockout.

Preheat oven to 350F (175C). Remove fat from lamb and discard. Slice garlic into thin slivers. With a very sharp knife, make small cuts all over the lamb—one for each sliver of garlic. Place one sliver into each cut. Using your hands, rub lamb with olive oil and sprinkle with salt and pepper. In a large pan over high heat, sear lamb quickly 5 to 10 minutes. In another large pan over medium heat, bring baby carrots, onions, white wine, beef broth, bay leaves, tomatoes, tomato sauce, pepper and salt to a boil. Transfer lamb into a roasting pan. Pour water into pan in which lamb has been seared, bring to a boil and add vegetable mixture. Reduce heat and cook 3 minutes. Pour over lamb in roasting pan. Place in oven and cook 4 hours, or until lamb is very tender. When lamb is done, transfer lamb from roasting pan to a platter. Discard bay leaves. Skim fat off cooking liquid. Place roasting pan with liquid over high heat and cook 3 to 5 minutes, or until much of the liquid has evaporated. Press vegetables through a strainer so that they become almost a puree. Arrange vegetable puree around lamb and serve.

Variation: Substitute 20 pearl onions for 6 medium-size ones.

Per Serving:

Calories: 380	*Total Fat: 9 g*	*Sat. Fat: 3 g*	*Chol.: 92 mg*

Italian Braised Leg of Lamb

Coscia di Montone all'Italiana

Serves: 8
Preparation Time: 15 minutes
Cooking Time: 3 to 4 hours

2 small onions
10 medium-size carrots
1 (4 - to 5-lb.) leg of lamb
2 tablespoons olive oil
2 garlic cloves, finely sliced
1 tablespoon dried rosemary
1/4 cup tomato paste
2 cups dry white wine

Cooking this aromatic dish will warm up your house with a mouthwatering smell.

Preheat oven to 400F (205C). Peel and cut onions into quarters and carrots into 2-inch rounds. Remove fat from lamb and discard. Place lamb in a large roasting pan. Pour olive oil over lamb and brown in oven 10 minutes. Reduce heat to 325F (165C). Add onions, carrots, garlic, rosemary and tomato paste to pan. Pour wine over lamb. Cover and bake 3 to 4 hours, basting every 20 minutes, or until brown all the way through and very tender. Place lamb on a platter. Skim fat off cooking liquid and serve as a sauce.

Variation: Beer or water can be used in place of wine, but for the best flavor, I prefer to use wine.

Hints: When basting, take lamb out of oven and close oven door so that temperature of the oven does not drop. When serving these leftovers remember that while in the refrigerator, fat will congeal, making it easy to remove from juice and scrape off lamb.

All'Italiana: Make sure not to waste a drop of delicious sauce—lavishly cover servings with it. Serve this dish with Rosemary Potatoes (page 126) and dunk Italian bread in the sauce.

Per Serving:
Calories: 484   Total Fat: 18 g   Sat. Fat: 6 g   Chol.: 164 mg

Lamb with Turnips

Agnello con Ravanelli

Serves: 6
Preparation Time: 20 minutes
Cooking Time: 2 hours

2 pounds lean lamb, cubed
2 tablespoons all-purpose flour
4 medium-size onions,
    quartered
1 pinch of dried marjoram
1 teaspoon dried leaf oregano
1 teaspoon dried rosemary
1 garlic clove, crushed
1/2 cup dry white wine
1 teaspoon salt
1 teaspoon pepper
2 pounds turnips, cubed
8 small red potatoes

Imagine a frosty evening. You put this dish on to cook slowly as you relax with a book by the fire. In time, your home will be filled with warm, rich smells and you will have a hearty meal.

In a large pan over medium heat, brown lamb in its own fat, several pieces at a time. When pieces become brown on all sides, remove from heat and continue until all lamb is browned. When all are brown, return to pan. Sprinkle lamb with flour and stir over medium heat 5 minutes. Add onions, herbs, garlic, wine, salt, pepper and enough water to almost cover. Bring to a boil. Reduce heat to low. Add turnips to lamb and cover. Simmer 1 hour. Cut unpeeled potatoes into small pieces. Add to lamb and cook 25 to 30 minutes, or until potatoes are tender.

All'Italiana: A take-off on traditional Irish stew, this Italian version goes down great with red wine and is a sure way to fight the cold-weather blues.

Per Serving:
Calories: 420   Total Fat: 9 g   Sat. Fat: 3 g   Chol.: 101 mg

Baked Leg of Lamb

Agnello al Forno

Serves: 10
Preparation Time: 10 minutes
Cooking Time: 1-1/2 to 1-3/4 hours

1 (5-lb.) leg of lamb
8 to 10 garlic cloves, or to taste
1 teaspoon salt
1 teaspoon pepper
1 tablespoon dried rosemary
1 tablespoon olive oil

Looks are deceiving. This elegant dish requires minimum fuss yet receives maximum praise.

Preheat oven to 375F (190C). Place lamb in a large roasting pan. With a sharp knife, make small cuts all around the meat. Cuts should be no deeper than 1/2 inch. Make 8 to 10 cuts, depending on how much garlic is to be used. Place one garlic clove in each cut. With your hands, rub salt, pepper and rosemary onto lamb and drizzle with olive oil. Roast 1-1/2 to 1-3/4 hours, or until dark brown on the outside, yet slightly pink on the inside. Let stand 10 minutes before carving.

All'Italiana: Serve with fava beans or lima beans on the side. The juice from the meat will run into the beans, making a succulent treat.

Per Serving:
Calories: 483   Total Fat: 31 g   Sat. Fat: 13 g   Chol.: 169 mg

Pork Chops Vernasca

Cotelette di Maiale alla Vernasca

Serves: 4
Preparation Time: 15 minutes
Cooking Time: 1-1/4 hours

4 (1-inch-thick) pork chops
2 ripe Bosc pears
1 teaspoon garlic powder
Pinch of salt
Pinch of pepper
1 tablespoon Dijon-style
    mustard
1/2 head cabbage (red or
    green), shredded
2 tablespoons brown sugar
1/2 cup dry white wine

*Pork doesn't have to be greasy or high in fat.
Today's pork is leaner than ever before.*

Preheat oven to 350F (175C). Trim fat off pork chops. Peel, remove cores and slice pears into 1/4-inch slices. Spray a large nonstick skillet with nonstick cooking spray. Add pork chops and cook over medium heat 10 minutes, or until golden-brown on both sides. Arrange in a shallow baking dish. In a small bowl, combine garlic powder, salt, pepper and mustard. With a brush, coat each pork chop with the mustard mixture. Add a layer of sliced pears. Cover with shredded cabbage. Sprinkle evenly with brown sugar. Pour white wine over dish. Bake 45 to 60 minutes, or until pork is white all the way through—no pink should remain.

Variation: Substitute 1/2 cup sauerkraut for shredded cabbage.

All'Italiana: To my mother's simple recipe for pork chops, I added Dijon mustard and cabbage—French and German touches I picked up from my wife and a friend who is a German chef.

Per Serving:
Calories: 278   Total Fat: 11 g   Sat. Fat: 3 g   Chol.: 63 mg

Braised Brisket of Beef

Brazato di Manzo di Mantova

Serves: 10
Preparation Time: 20 minutes
Cooking Time: 2-1/2 to 3 hours

1 (5- to 6-lb.) beef brisket
1 (10-oz.) can condensed tomato soup
1 cup beef broth
2 cups water
1 cup chopped carrots
1 cup chopped celery
1 cup chopped onions
1 tablespoon grated dried porcini mushrooms (optional)
1 cup grated Parmesan cheese (3 ounces) (optional)

This was a favorite of Mrs. Jacob Javitz. I made it at every gathering I catered for her and the Senator.

On fatty side of brisket, cut as many lengthwise slits into brisket that fit about 1 inch apart. In a large roasting pan, combine tomato soup, beef broth and water. Place brisket into pan, fat-side up. In a blender set to high speed or a food processor equipped with the metal blade, process carrots, celery and onions until smooth. Spread vegetable puree on brisket. Bake 2-1/2 to 3 hours, basting every 20 minutes, or until very tender. Add a little water if liquid reduces too much. When brisket is done, trim off excess fat from top with a sharp knife. If using mushroom/cheese topping: In a food processor equipped with the metal blade, or by hand, chop dried mushrooms until very fine—as if they were grated. Combine mushrooms and Parmesan cheese and sprinkle on top of finished brisket and serve. Or serve mushroom mixture separately for guests to sprinkle to their liking. Skim fat from cooking liquid and serve as a sauce.

All'Italiana: A typical way to enjoy this unique beef dish is to serve it with plain cooked ziti. The ziti will soak up the rich juices from the meat. Complement this masterpiece with a robust dry red wine.

Per Serving:

Calories: 470   *Total Fat: 25 g*   *Sat. Fat: 10 g*   *Chol.: 153 mg*

Veal Scaloppine with Peppers

Scaloppine di Vitello coi Peperoni

Serves: 4
Preparation Time: 10 minutes
Cooking Time: 16 minutes

2 tablespoons all-purpose flour
4 veal scallopine from range-fed
   veal
1 tablespoon olive oil
3/4 cup dry white wine
1/2 cup chopped green bell
   pepper
1/2 cup chopped red bell
   pepper
1 teaspoon garlic powder
1/4 teaspoon salt
1/4 teaspoon black pepper
1/4 teaspoon ground nutmeg

Many of my clients now request that I use only range-fed veal. Ask your butcher for it.

Pour flour onto a plate. Dip veal in flour until lightly and evenly coated. In a large nonstick skillet over medium heat, heat olive oil. Add veal and sauté until golden-brown on both sides. Add remaining ingredients and cover. Reduce heat and simmer 8 to 10 minutes.

All'Italiana: Take a hint from the *trattorias* of Italy—serve these scallopines on top of spaghetti. Plain white rice also works well.

Per Serving:
Calories: 273   Total Fat: 12 g   Sat. Fat: 3 g   Chol.: 93 mg

Veal Piccata

Vitello Piccata

Serves: 4 to 8
Preparation Time: 15 minutes
Cooking Time: 10 minutes

8 veal scallopine from range-fed
   veal
1/4 cup all-purpose flour
1/4 cup olive oil
1 lemon, halved
1 teaspoon capers
2 tablespoons chopped parsley

This is a quintessential veal dish that is popular throughout Italy.

Arrange veal between 2 sheets of waxed paper. With a kitchen mallet, pound veal until very thin. Pour flour onto a plate. Remove waxed paper. Dip veal in flour until lightly and evenly coated. In a large pan over high heat, heat olive oil. Add veal and cook quickly, 3 to 5 minutes on each side. Remove veal and arrange on a platter. Squeeze lemon juice into pan and stir quickly. Pour over veal. Sprinkle with capers and parsley and serve.

Variation: Substitute thinly sliced boneless turkey breasts for veal.

All'Italiana: I have learned from the greatest Italian chefs that it is essential to get the pan very hot before cooking veal. So hot, that you will be, in fact, almost searing the meat.

Per Serving:
Calories: 290   Total Fat: 18 g   Sat. Fat: 4 g   Chol.: 93 mg

Veal Scallopine with Mushrooms

Scallopine di Vitello con Funghi

Serves: 6
Preparation Time: 15 minutes
Cooking Time: 35 minutes

10 veal scallopine from range-fed veal
4 tablespoons all-purpose flour
1/2 ounce dried porcini mushrooms
3 tablespoons margarine
1/2 cup plain nonfat yogurt
1 tablespoon brandy
Salt and pepper to taste

Veal with mushrooms is a favorite of mine because it combines two delicate tastes and textures.

Preheat oven to 400F (205C). Arrange veal between 2 sheets of waxed paper. With a kitchen mallet, pound veal until very thin. Pour 3 tablespoons of the flour onto a plate. Remove waxed paper. Dip veal in flour until lightly and evenly coated. In a small pan over medium heat, bring dried porcini mushrooms to a boil in enough water to cover. Remove from heat. Let stand in water until ready for use. In a medium-size nonstick skillet over medium heat, melt margarine. Add 4 to 5 veal scallopine at a time (or however many will fit snugly). Cook 3 to 4 minutes on each side, or until scallopine look quite shiny and golden. Remove scallopine when done and cook the rest. Arrange veal scallopine on a sheet of foil, at least 12 inches long. Drain porcini mushrooms. Set aside. To same pan in which veal was cooked, stir in remaining flour and cook 1 to 2 minutes, or until foamy. Stir in yogurt, brandy and mushrooms and reduce heat. Add salt and pepper to taste. Stir and cook 3 to 5 minutes, or until sauce thickens. Pour over veal scallopine and fold foil over them and close tightly. Bake 10 minutes. Remove from oven and open package carefully. Arrange veal scallopine on serving platter and cover with mushroom sauce.

All'Italiana: Serve this wonderful dish over plain white rice. The rice will soak up the delicious sauce.

Per Serving:
Calories: 224   Total Fat: 11 g   Sat. Fat: 3 g   Chol.: 94 mg

Pasta

Italian cooking is multidimensional, and nowhere is this more evident than in pasta dishes. Fettucini alla Vodka e Salmone (page 81) and Paglia e Fieno al Yogurt (page 92) demonstrate the flair for transforming regional and global ingredients into undeniably Italian masterpieces. Spaghetti alla Checca (page 94) showcases three quintessential Italian ingredients, Penne Puttanesca (page 84) highlights regional delicacies and Spaghetti alla Carbonara (page 83) boasts a rich history. Penne con Broccoli e Pangrattato (page 80) and Penne con Salsa di Noci (page 86) illustrate the ability Italian home-cooking has for making simple ingredients come alive with fantastic flavor. Ziti con Salsa di Tacchino in Forno (page 79) utilizes turkey, which is naturally low in fat and cholesterol. These recipes and the others in this section are simple to make, low in cholesterol and fat and are sure to become favorites of yours as they are of mine.

I remember when I used to carry my pasta machine to every party I catered because homemade was the operative word in preparing succulent and memorable pasta dishes. Today, there are fresh pastas available in the refrigerated sections of supermarkets and many packaged varieties of dry pasta are wonderful. Now at most parties, as well as at home, I use these varieties with the same success I enjoyed with homemade pasta.

Spaghetti with Anchovies

Spaghetti con le Acciughe

Serves: 4
Preparation Time: 15 minutes
Cooking Time: 15 minutes

8 ounces spaghetti
10 to 13 anchovy fillets
1/2 cup olive oil
Salt and pepper to taste
1/2 teaspoon capers (optional)
1/2 teaspoon hot red pepper
   flakes (optional)

This dish is a quickie—invented to indulge an anchovy lover's passion!

Cook spaghetti according to package directions until al dente. Reserve 1/2 cup of cooking water as you drain spaghetti. Set spaghetti aside and keep your pan handy. In a blender set to medium speed or a food processor equipped with the metal blade, process anchovy fillets with cooking water and olive oil until ingredients form a thick, smooth paste. With a rubber spatula, transfer ingredients into pot. Toss in spaghetti. Cook and stir over low heat until paste is well blended into spaghetti. Do not boil. Season with salt and pepper, keeping in mind that anchovy fillets are very salty. Stir in capers and/or red pepper flakes, if using.

All'Italiana: It is customary in Italy not to sprinkle Parmesan or Romano cheese on pasta prepared with seafood. Take your cue from the pros and refrain—just enjoy the delicious anchovy flavor.

Per Serving:
Calories: 231   Total Fat: 2 g   Sat. Fat: 0.3 g   Chol.: 9 mg

Ziti in Succulent Turkey Sauce

Ziti con Salsa di Tacchino in Forno

Serves: 6
Preparation Time: 20 minutes
Cooking Time: 30 minutes

3 garlic cloves, minced
1 medium-size red onion,
   coarsely chopped
1 tablespoon dried leaf basil
1 pinch of dried leaf marjoram
1/2 pound ground turkey
   (white meat, no skin)
1 tablespoon olive oil
1/2 cup dry white wine
1 tablespoon red wine vinegar
10 ounces ziti
2 cups Classic Tomato Sauce
   (page 141) or commercial
   tomato pasta sauce
1/4 teaspoon salt
1/4 teaspoon black pepper
1 teaspoon hot red pepper
   flakes, or to taste
1 cup shredded part-skim
   mozzarella cheese (4 ounces)
1 tablespoon grated Parmesan
   cheese

This is a favorite among many of my clients in Palm Beach. They love it so much that I have to make two batches of the dish, one for dinner and one for them to enjoy the next day.

In a medium-size bowl, mix garlic, onion, basil and marjoram into turkey. In a medium-size pan over medium heat, heat olive oil. Add turkey mixture and sauté 5 minutes or until mixture is dry and turkey is no longer pink. Stir in wine and vinegar. Cook 3 minutes. While meat is cooking, in a large pot cook ziti according to package directions until al dente. Preheat oven to 400F (205C). Reduce heat under turkey mixture and stir in tomato sauce, salt, black pepper and pepper flakes. Simmer 10 minutes. Drain cooked ziti and pour into a shallow baking dish. Add turkey sauce. Mix well so that ziti is covered in sauce. Sprinkle mozzarella cheese, then Parmesan cheese over dish. Bake 10 minutes, or until top is crispy.

Variations: Water can be used instead of white wine. About 1/4 cup chopped fresh basil can be substituted for dried basil.

All'Italiana: In Italy this dish would be enjoyed for lunch, accompanied by a rich red wine and followed by a wonderful, noon-day siesta.

Per Serving:
Calories: 350   Total Fat: 9 g   Sat. Fat: 3 g   Chol.: 39 mg

Penne with Broccoli & Bread Crumbs

Penne con Broccoli e Pangrattato

Serves: 6
Preparation Time: 5 minutes
Cooking Time: 20 minutes

1 bunch broccoli
10 ounces penne
1/2 cup olive oil
3 garlic cloves, crushed
3/4 cup coarse plain bread
    crumbs, crushed
Salt and pepper to taste

A unique peasant recipe that is a great switch from spicy, saucy pasta dishes.

Cut broccoli into bite-size pieces. Stems should be used too, just peel off the hard outer part and chop the tender part into small pieces. Cook penne according to package directions until al dente. In a separate pan, cook broccoli in enough water to cover until tender. Drain penne, reserving 1 cup of cooking water. Drain broccoli and set aside. Set penne and water aside. In a large pan over medium heat, heat olive oil. Add garlic and sauté 3 minutes, or until translucent. Do not let garlic brown. If it does, quickly stir in 1/4 cup of reserved water to reduce heat. Stir in bread crumbs until liquid is absorbed. Stir in cooked broccoli. Toss in penne. Season with salt and pepper. Remove from heat when penne and sauce are well blended and hot. Stir in enough of the reserved water to make sauce the correct consistency.

Variation: Try 1/2 pound broccoli with 1/2 pound yellow zucchini for more color.

All'Italiana: My mother used to make this when the family was tired of tomato sauce. Many Italians choose a sauce such as this for the same reason.

Per Serving:
Calories: 400   Total Fat: 19 g   Sat. Fat: 3 g   Chol.: 0 mg

Spiked Fettucini with Salmon

Fettucine alla Vodka e Salmone

Serves: 4
Preparation Time: 10 minutes
Cooking Time: 30 minutes

1/4 pound salmon fillet
8 ounces fettucini
1/4 cup reduced-fat cream
    cheese
1 cup chicken broth
1/2 cup grated Parmesan
    cheese (2-1/4 ounces)
2 tablespoons vodka

A real show-stopper! This was a hit at the Palm Beach home of Jack Massey, the owner of Kentucky Fried Chicken.

Cut salmon fillet into 2" X 1" pieces. Cook fettucini according to package directions until al dente. Drain fettucini, saving 1 cup of cooking water. Set aside. In a large saucepan over medium heat, melt cream cheese with chicken broth. Bring to a boil, stir in salmon, Parmesan cheese and vodka. Reduce heat and simmer until salmon is light pink and begins to flake when you pierce it with a fork. If sauce is too thick, stir in some of the reserved cooking water. Pour fettucini into a serving dish. Cover with sauce and serve.

Variation: Instead of cream cheese, stir 1/2 teaspoon cornstarch into a little of the cold chicken broth. Continue as above.

All'Italiana: A perfect prelude to this elegant dish is a typical green salad made with arugala, tomatoes and radicchio. Your table will be awash in color.

Per Serving:
Calories: 385   Total Fat: 12 g   Sat. Fat: 5 g   Chol.: 92 mg

Pasta Shells with Vegetables

Conchiglie Ortolane

Serves: 4
Preparation Time: 10 minutes
Cooking Time: 20 minutes

2 medium-size Italian eggplants
2 medium-size zucchini
10 ounces pasta shells
1 cup green peas (fresh or
    frozen)
2 tablespoons olive oil
1 cup Classic Tomato Sauce
    (page 141) or purchased
    tomato pasta sauce
Salt and pepper to taste

A delicate dish that will usher in spring—even if it's the middle of February. Kathy Ford, wife of the late Henry Ford II, loved this dish served poolside in Palm Beach.

Peel eggplant and cut into 1/2-inch cubes. Cut zucchini into 1/2-inch cubes. Cook pasta shells according to package directions until al dente. In a small pan over medium heat, cook peas in 2 cups water until tender. Drain and set aside. In a medium-size nonstick skillet over medium heat, heat olive oil. Add zucchini and eggplant and sauté 3 to 5 minutes or until zucchini is translucent and eggplant is browned. Toss pasta shells into skillet with eggplant and zucchini and stir. Stir in peas and cook 1 minute. Stir in tomato sauce. Reduce heat. Season with salt and pepper. Simmer 5 minutes, but do not boil.

Variation: Serve with a side dish of Parmesan or Romano cheese for guests to add as desired.

All'Italiana: Sometimes I substitute chickpeas (garbonzos) for green peas for a decidedly more authentic Italian taste.

Per Serving:
Calories: 368   Total Fat: 8 g   Sat. Fat: 1 g   Chol.: 0 mg

Mountain Man Spaghetti

Spaghetti alla Carbonara

Serves: 6
Preparation Time: 10 minutes
Cooking Time: 20 minutes

8 ounces spaghetti
3 egg whites
1/4 cup grated Parmesan
   cheese (2-1/4 ounces)
1/2 tablespoon pepper
1 pinch of dried leaf marjoram
1 pinch of dried leaf oregano
1/4 cup olive oil
3 garlic cloves, finely chopped

This dish is named for the carbonari, men who worked in the mountains making wood into charcoal. To sustain themselves they carried with them dried pasta, spices and cheese and relied on generous farmers to give them fresh eggs.

Cook spaghetti according to package directions until al dente. Drain and keep hot. In a medium-size bowl, combine egg whites, Parmesan cheese, pepper, marjoram and oregano and set aside. In a large pan over medium heat, heat olive oil. Add garlic and sauté 3 minutes, or until golden. Do not brown. Remove from heat. Transfer hot spaghetti into a serving bowl. Pour egg mixture and garlic mixture over spaghetti. Toss well and serve hot.

Variations: Romano cheese can be substituted for Parmesan cheese. Also, 1/2 cup liquid egg substitute can be used instead of egg whites.

All'Italiana: This hearty dish stands well on its own or as a prelude to Roasted Chicken (page 51).

Per Serving:
Calories: 268   Total Fat: 12 g   Sat. Fat: 3 g   Chol.: 7 mg

Penne with Spicy Anchovy Sauce

Penne Puttanesca

Serves: 4
Preparation Time: 20 minutes
Cooking Time: 20 minutes

10 ounces penne
4 garlic cloves
10 to 12 anchovy fillets
2 cups chopped tomatoes
   (fresh or canned)
3 tablespoons capers, drained
1 pinch dried leaf marjoram
1/4 teaspoon hot red pepper
   flakes
2 tablespoons olive oil
Salt and black pepper to taste
1/2 cup ripe olives, coarsely
   chopped

Italian food doesn't get much hotter than this! The first dish I prepared for my class in Italian cooking at the America-Italy Society in New York, this recipe will always be a favorite of mine.

Cook penne according to package directions until al dente. While penne cooks, in a blender or a food processor equipped with the metal blade, process garlic 10 seconds or until finely chopped. Stop machine and add anchovies and tomatoes. Process 5 seconds. Add capers, marjoram, pepper flakes and olive oil and process 5 seconds more or until mixture forms a thick, smooth paste. Do not over-process or mixture will become soupy. Pour mixture into a large pan and simmer, uncovered, over low heat 10 to 12 minutes. Reduce heat if mixture begins to boil. Drain penne and reserve 1 cup cooking water. Spoon out some sauce and set aside in small bowl for garnishing. Add drained penne to large pan containing sauce and stir over very low heat. If sauce is too thick, slowly pour in enough reserved cooking water to make the sauce the desired consistency. Season with salt and pepper. Serve when sauce and penne are well blended. Transfer penne to a platter and garnish with reserved sauce and olives.

All'Italiana: This dish goes perfectly with a nice Barbera wine. I recently tried my first California Barbera and it was as good as any Italian I've tried.

Per Serving:
Calories: 395   Total Fat: 12 g   Sat. Fat: 2 g   Chol.: 9 mg

Penne with Tomato, Basil & Garlic

Penne alla Checca di Porto Santo Stefano

Serves: 6
Preparation Time: 1-1/2 hours including refrigeration time
Cooking Time: 15 minutes

4 cups chopped tomatoes (canned or fresh)
30 fresh basil leaves (don't use dried basil)
3 garlic cloves
1-1/2 cups shredded part-skim mozzarella cheese (6 ounces)
1 teaspoon salt
1 teaspoon pepper
1/3 cup olive oil
10 ounces penne

The tiny village of Porto Santo Stefano is a popular vacation spot for Romans and a place close to my family's heart.

Place tomatoes in a large bowl. Finely chop basil and garlic and mix into tomatoes. Stir in cheese, salt, pepper and oil. Refrigerate 1 hour. Cook penne according to package directions until al dente. Drain penne and return to its pan. Add tomato mixture to penne and blend well. Cook over low heat, stirring, until dish is hot and cheese is melted, but be careful mozzarella cheese does not burn. Serve very hot because, as it cools, the cheese will harden.

All'Italiana: Serve with thick slices of Italian bread for friends to lap up remaining sauce. *Delizioso!*

Per Serving:
Calories: 390   Total Fat: 17 g   Sat. Fat: 5 g   Chol.: 16 mg

Penne with Walnut Sauce

Penne con Salsa di Noci

Serves: 6
Preparation Time: 10 minutes
Cooking Time: 15 minutes

10 ounces penne
3 garlic cloves
3/4 cup walnuts, coarsely
   chopped
1/4 cup olive oil
1/4 cup grated Parmesan
   cheese

A real exotic treat, but a cinch to whip up. When they were growing up, my daughters loved this dish because of its nutty flavor.

Cook penne according to package directions until al dente. Drain penne, reserving 1 cup of the cooking water. Set penne and water aside in separate bowls. In a small food processor equipped with the metal blade, process garlic, chopped walnuts, olive oil and Parmesan cheese 10 seconds, or until finely chopped. Return penne to its pan and add sauce. Cook over low heat, stirring, until penne and sauce are hot and blended. If sauce is too thick, slowly stir in a little reserved water. Serve hot.

All'Italiana: This is a favorite in Italy during the winter months when many fresh vegetables are not in season. I loved to fix this for my family on cold winter nights.

Per Serving:
Calories: 276   Total Fat: 11 g   Sat. Fat: 2 g   Chol.: 3 mg

Penne with Eggplant

Penne con Melanzane

Serves: 4
Preparation Time: 10 minutes
Cooking Time: 30 to 35 minutes

12 ounces penne
1 medium-size Italian eggplant
3 tablespoons olive oil
1 small onion, coarsely chopped
1/2 cup thinly sliced white mushrooms (optional)
1-1/2 cups Classic Tomato Sauce (page 141) or purchased tomato pasta sauce
1 teaspoon dried leaf basil
1 dried bay leaf
1 teaspoon dried leaf oregano
1/4 cup dry red wine
1/2 cup shredded part-skim mozzarella cheese (2 ounces)
Salt and pepper to taste

Along with pasta, pizza and delicious cheeses, Italians brought their eggplant to America. Well, there's more to eggplant than parmigiana.

Cook penne according to package directions until al dente. Drain, reserving 1/2 cup of the cooking water. Set both penne and water aside. Peel eggplant and cut into 1/2-inch cubes. In a large nonstick pan over medium heat, heat 2 tablespoons of the olive oil. Add eggplant and sauté 5 minutes, or until browned and translucent. Transfer eggplant into a bowl. Set aside. In same large pan over medium heat, add remaining olive oil and sauté onions and mushrooms 3 minutes, or until onion is translucent and mushrooms are darkish-brown. Stir in cooked eggplant, tomato sauce, basil, bay leaf, oregano and wine. Cook 10 minutes more, reducing heat if mixture begins to boil. If sauce is too thick, slowly pour in a little reserved water. Remove bay leaf and discard. Stir in penne and cheese. Cook, stirring, until cheese has melted. Season with salt and pepper. Serve hot.

Hint: I find that if I use canned tomato pasta sauce, it often makes the sauce too salty. An old Italian trick to make sauce less salty and sweeter is to add a pinch of sugar. Add a pinch, stir it in and taste. Keep adding sugar until the bite of saltiness is gone. Another Italian method is to grate a carrot into the sauce. Again, taste as you go and use only as much carrot as you need to take away the salty taste and give your sauce a sweet flavor.

All'Italiana: Add grated carrot to the tomato-based sauce to add a sweet, tangy flavor.

Per Serving:

Calories: 488   Total Fat: 14 g   Sat. Fat: 3 g   Chol.: 8 mg

Spaghetti with Walnuts

Spaghetti e Noci

Serves: 6
Preparation Time: 15 minutes
Cooking Time: 20 minutes

8 ounces spaghetti
1-1/2 cups walnuts, coarsely
    chopped
1 cup coarsely chopped white
    Italian bread (with crust)
Salt and pepper to taste

Invite guests over for an authentic Italian meal and they'll expect a tomato or a cream sauce. Throw them a curve and serve up this delectable, offbeat but thoroughly Italian dish.

Cook spaghetti according to package directions until al dente. While spaghetti is cooking, in a food processor equipped with the metal blade, process chopped walnuts and Italian bread 30 seconds, or until finely chopped. Transfer into a large bowl and season with salt and pepper. Set aside. Drain spaghetti and reserve 1/2 cup of the cooking water. Stir reserved water into walnut mixture. Toss in spaghetti and season with salt and pepper. Serve hot.

All'Italiana: A classic, this is

served in Italy as a change

from tomato-sauced dishes,

especially during the winter

months when many fresh

vegetables are not in season.

Per Serving:
Calories: 390   Total Fat: 19 g   Sat. Fat: 2 g   Chol.: 0 mg

Tagliatelle with Ricotta & Walnuts

Tagliatelle con Ricotta e Noci

Serves: 6
Preparation Time: 10 minutes
Cooking Time: 15 minutes

10 ounces tagliatelle
1/4 cup olive oil
1/2 cup walnuts, coarsely
   chopped
1 cup part-skim ricotta cheese
2 to 4 tablespoons grated
   Parmesan cheese

This dish combines the rich texture of walnuts with the sweet taste of ricotta.

Cook tagliatelle according to package directions until al dente. Drain. Set aside. In same pan over low heat, combine all ingredients except Parmesan cheese and tagliatelle. Stir frequently and bring to a gentle boil. Add tagliatelle and stir until well blended. Sprinkle with Parmesan cheese and serve hot.

All'Italiana: This dish highlights two beloved tastes and textures of Italian cuisine: ricotta cheese and walnuts. It goes as well with a nice Orvieto or Pinot Grigio as it does with a hearty Chianti.

Per Serving:
Calories: 385   Total Fat: 21 g   Sat. Fat: 4 g   Chol.: 58 mg

Penne with Turkey Sausage

Penne con Salciccia Affumicata

Serves: 4
Preparation Time: 5 minutes
Cooking Time: 20 minutes

8 ounces penne
1 pound turkey sausage, chopped
1 cup Chianti or other red wine
1/2 teaspoon hot red pepper flakes
1/2 teaspoon black pepper

This is a terrific way to use turkey sausage, which is just as spicy and succulent as beef or pork sausage but does not contain as much fat and cholesterol.

Cook penne according to package directions until al dente. While penne is cooking, in a large nonstick pan over high heat, sauté turkey sausage 5 minutes. Remove from heat and discard any fat. Add red wine to turkey in pan. Bring to a boil over medium heat. Reduce heat and simmer 5 minutes. Drain penne and add to turkey mixture. Stir in pepper flakes and black pepper and serve.

All'Italiana: Delight in this special meal with a chilled Fontana Candida or Frascati.

Per Serving:
Calories: 492   Total Fat: 17 g   Sat. Fat: 0.1 g   Chol.: 100 mg

Pasta with Ricotta & Spinach Filling

Cannelloni

Serves: 6
Preparation Time: 15 minutes
Cooking Time: 40 minutes

2 (10-oz.) packages frozen chopped spinach
14 cannelloni tubes
15 ounces part-skim ricotta cheese
1/2 cup liquid egg substitute
1 pinch of nutmeg
2 tablespoons grated Parmesan cheese
1 cup thinly sliced white mushrooms
1 medium-size onion, coarsely chopped
1 tablespoon lemon juice
1 cup Classic Tomato Sauce (page 141) or purchased tomato pasta sauce
1/2 cup shredded part-skim mozzarella cheese (2 ounces)

All'Italiana: This is a very filling meal, one I love best when accompanied by a simple salad made with Bibb lettuce, endive and arugala.

A favorite at most Italian restaurants and a hit with kids. The creamy filling is wrapped in a delicate pasta tube and covered in a succulent tomato sauce.

Cook spinach according to package directions. Drain excess water from spinach and set aside. Cook cannelloni according to package directions until al dente. Drain and set aside. Preheat oven to 400F (205C). In a large bowl, combine ricotta cheese, spinach, egg substitute, nutmeg and Parmesan cheese. Spray a shallow baking dish with nonstick cooking spray. Using a teaspoon or pastry bag, fill cooked cannelloni tubes from end to end with filling. (Do not overfill, as filling will expand a bit.) Lay cannelloni side by side in prepared baking dish. Set aside. In large pan over medium heat, cook mushrooms and onion with lemon juice 3 minutes, or until onion is translucent and mushrooms are tender. Reduce heat if mushrooms and onion brown too quickly. Pour mushrooms and onion over cannelloni. Cover with tomato sauce and sprinkle with mozzarella cheese. Bake 15 minutes or until cheese is melted and edges are crispy.

Variations: Substitute 1-1/2 pounds fresh spinach for frozen spinach. Instead of egg substitute, use 2 egg whites.

Note: Nutmeg a is very strong spice, so make your pinch tiny.

Per Serving:
Calories: 360   Total Fat: 10 g   Sat. Fat: 5 g   Chol.: 65 mg

Spinach Tagliatelle with Ham & Yogurt

Paglia e Fieno al Yogurt

Serves: 4
Preparation Time: 10 minutes
Cooking Time: 20 minutes

1/4 pound boiled lean ham
10 ounces spinach tagliatelle
2 tablespoons olive oil
1 cup baby green peas (fresh, frozen or canned)
1-1/2 cups plain nonfat yogurt

Yogurt lends a light and creamy texture to this simple and simply delicious pasta dish. This was one of Joan Fontaine's favorites when I cooked for her in New York .

Cut ham into julienne strips. Cook tagliatelle according to package directions until al dente. Drain tagliatelle and set aside. Over medium heat, in same pan used for tagliatelle, heat oil. Add ham and sauté 1 minute. Add peas and cook 3 to 5 minutes, or until hot. Stir in yogurt. Toss in tagliatelle and serve.

Variation: I prefer to enjoy this dish without adding spices. But feel free to experiment with some of your favorite spices to make the dish uniquely yours.

All'Italiana: If you love Tagliatelle Alfredo, you'll love this version which eliminates much of the fat and cholesterol. Try it with a chilled Bardolino or Valpolicella wine.

Per Serving:
Calories: 450   Total Fat: 11 g   Sat. Fat: 2 g   Chol.: 79 mg

92

Angel Hair Pasta with Turkey

Spaghettini con Tacchino

Serves: 4
Preparation Time: 10 minutes
Cooking Time: 15 minutes

8 ounces angel hair pasta
1/4 cup parsley
1/4 cup fresh basil
1 cup Tofunetta (page 132)
1 garlic clove
3/4 cup skim milk
2 tablespoons olive oil
1/4 pound ground turkey
   (white meat only, no skin)

The perfect way to enjoy angel hair pasta is with fragrant herbs and the light texture and taste of turkey.

Cook pasta according to package directions until al dente. Drain and reserve 1 cup of the cooking water. Set both pasta and water aside. In a blender set to low speed or a food processor equipped with the metal blade, process parsley, basil, Tofunetta, garlic and skim milk 10 seconds, or until smooth. Over medium heat, in same pan used to cook pasta, heat olive oil. Add turkey and sauté 3 minutes. Slowly stir in blended ingredients. Bring to a gentle boil and add pasta. If sauce is too thick, slowly stir in a little reserved cooking water. Serve hot.

All'Italiana: This typically Italian way of serving up delicate flavors goes best with a crisp Orvieto or Pinot Grigio wine.

Per Serving:
Calories: 374   Total Fat: 13 g   Sat. Fat: 2 g   Chol.: 75 mg

Spaghetti with Tomato, Basil & Yogurt

Spaghetti alla Checca

Serves: 6
Preparation Time: 20 minutes
Cooking Time: 20 minutes

12 ounces spaghetti
3 very ripe Roma tomatoes
1/2 cup fresh basil
1-1/2 cups shredded part-skim
    mozzarella cheese (6
    ounces)
1/4 cup grated Parmesan
    cheese
1/4 cup parsley, chopped
2 garlic cloves
2 tablespoons olive oil
1 cup plain nonfat yogurt
1/2 teaspoon salt

Nonfat yogurt adds creaminess to the classic Checca recipe.

Cook spaghetti according to package directions until al dente. Drain and set aside. Remove skin and seeds from tomatoes and cut flesh into small cubes. Set aside. Separate basil leaves from stems and bruise. Set aside. In a large bowl, mix together mozzarella and Parmesan cheeses. Set aside. By hand, or in a small food processor equipped with the metal blade, finely chop together parsley and garlic. In a large pan over medium heat, cook parsley and garlic mixture in olive oil 3 to 5 minutes. Do not let garlic brown. Add tomatoes and basil and bring to a boil. Stir in yogurt and salt. Bring sauce to a boil and stir in spaghetti and cheese mixture. Pour spaghetti onto a platter and serve immediately.

Variations: Instead of using fresh tomatoes, use 1 (16-oz.) can drained Roma tomatoes. Substitute 2 tablespoons dried basil for fresh basil, but soak dried basil in 1/2 cup water for 1/2 hour before using. Use 1 cup Tofunetta (page 132) instead of yogurt.

All'Italiana: This recipe illustrates how Italy takes the newest ingredients, from yogurt to tofu, and creates a taste that is uniquely Italian.

Per Serving:
Calories: 352   Total Fat: 11 g   Sat. Fat: 3 g   Chol.: 12 mg

Tagliatelle with Tuna & Peas

Tagliatelle con Tonno e Piselli

Serves: 6
Preparation Time: 10 minutes
Cooking Time: 15 to 20 minutes

16 ounces tagliatelle
1 (6-1/8-oz.) can white albacore tuna packed in oil
1 cup baby green peas (fresh, frozen or canned)
1/4 teaspoon black pepper
1 tablespoon margarine, room temperature
3 tablespoons finely chopped parsley

Tuna casserole again? Try this light but hearty dish instead.

Cook tagliatelle according to package directions until al dente, drain and set aside. In a medium-size pan over low heat, simmer tuna in its own oil. With a wooden spoon or fork, break up tuna into bite-size pieces and cook 2 to 3 minutes. Do not burn. Add peas and pepper. Simmer 3 minutes. Spoon margarine into a serving bowl and set aside. Add parsley to pan and simmer 1 minute. Remove from heat and pour tuna sauce into serving bowl with margarine. Add tagliatelle and toss well enough for margarine to melt completely.

All'Italiana: This is a spring dish, so serve it with a fruity white wine such as Frascati.

Per Serving:
Calories: 377   Total Fat: 7 g   Sat. Fat: 1.0 g   Chol.: 80 mg

Polenta e Riso

Polenta & Rice

Northern Italians enjoy polenta like Southern Italians love pasta. When things were tough after World War II, wives and mothers in the North would prepare polenta every day and in many cases it took the place of meat as the main part of the meal. Vegetables, cheese, herbs—almost any ingredient they had—would be added to polenta to transform it into a satisfying dinner.

I have collected my favorite recipes, which utilize richly flavored cheeses such as fontina, ricotta and Gorgonzola, and fresh vegetables such as broccoli. Polenta is delicious and nutritious, low in fat and cholesterol, even when prepared with cheese. These days, precooked polenta is available in many supermarkets and specialty stores. Try it once and soon you'll be adding your own favorite ingredients like my mother did.

Rice is another bedrock of Northern Italian cooking, especially risotto, the creamy rice dishes that are turning up at more and more Italian restaurants here in America. Rice and risotto are as important in Northern Italy as macaroni is in Naples, and just as versatile. The recipes listed here utilize mushrooms, beans, pumpkin and squash, among other ingredients, to add a distinct Northern Italian flavor. One example even utilizes vodka to show the international flair risotto can have.

Basic Polenta

Polenta Semplice

Serves: 8
Preparation Time: 20 minutes
Cooking Time: 1-1/2 hours

2 quarts plus 1 cup water
1 teaspoon salt
2 cups yellow cornmeal

Polenta from scratch is delicious, but unfortunately it requires a strong arm to do all the stirring that is needed. You may opt to try store-bought, precooked polenta.

In a large pot, bring the 2 quarts water and salt to a boil. Reduce heat to low. With one hand, slowly pour in cornmeal. Stir vigorously with the other hand. As the polenta begins to thicken, stir more slowly. Stop stirring and cook over low heat 30 minutes. In a small pot, bring the 1 cup water to a boil. Add boiling water to cornmeal mixture and stir. Transfer cornmeal mixture to the top part of a double boiler and cook over low heat 1 hour, keeping water at a simmer. Pour out polenta on a damp, clean, flat surface such as a foil-lined countertop, baking sheet or a wooden board. Spray a wooden spoon with nonstick cooking spray to prevent polenta from sticking and use it to spread polenta 1 inch thick. Cut into small circles with a cookie cutter or slice for use in polenta recipes. Makes about 10 cups.

Hint: Leftover polenta can be refrigerated up to 3 days or frozen for longer storage. Commercial precooked polenta is available in packages in stores that stock Italian and Spanish foods.

All'Italiana: Polenta is wonderful with cooked vegetables such as broccoli or beans mixed right in. Polenta is a staple of Northern Italian cooking, and once you try it, you'll see why.

Per Serving:
Calories: 105   Total Fat: 1 g   Sat. Fat: 0.1 g   Chol.: 0 mg

Baked Polenta with Fontina Cheese

Polenta al Forno con Fontina

Serves: 8
Preparation Time: 15 minutes
with precooked polenta
Cooking Time: 30 minutes

3 cups purchased precooked
polenta or cooked Basic
Polenta (page 98)
1/2 pound Italian fontina
cheese, thinly sliced
2 tablespoons grated Parmesan
cheese
2 tablespoons margarine

This dish will warm you from the inside out. Prepare it on a winter's night and laugh at the snow burying your car outside.

Preheat oven to 400F (205C). Spray a nonstick baking dish or pie pan with nonstick cooking spray. Add a 1/4-inch-thick layer of precooked polenta. Cover polenta with thin layer of cheese. Cover cheese with a layer of polenta and continue until all polenta and cheese have been used and the top layer of the dish is polenta. (As dish sizes can vary in this recipe, the number of layers will vary—it is okay to have 2 layers of polenta and 1 layer of cheese). Sprinkle with Parmesan cheese. Dot with teaspoons of margarine. Bake 30 minutes, or until top is golden.

All'Italiana: Only Italian fontina cheese will work. Serve this dish with a hearty red wine and enjoy a satisfying meal.

Per Serving:
Calories: 222   Total Fat: 13 g   Sat. Fat: 6 g   Chol.: 34 mg

Polenta with Broccoli & Gorgonzola Cheese

Polenta con Broccoli e Gorgonzola

Serves: 4
Preparation Time: 5 minutes
with precooked polenta
Cooking Time: 15 minutes

2 cups cold water
1 cup purchased precooked
    polenta or cooked Basic
    Polenta (page 98)
1/4 teaspoon salt
1/4 teaspoon pepper
1 cup coarsely chopped
    broccoli
1 cup crumbled Gorgonzola
    cheese (4 ounces)

The lightest dish that will ever stick to your ribs. The combination of cheese, broccoli and polenta is deliciously filling.

Pour cold water into a medium-size pan over medium heat. Stir in precooked polenta. Add salt and pepper and bring to a boil. Gently stir in broccoli. Reduce heat and simmer 5 to 6 minutes, or until broccoli is tender. Using a rubber spatula or a wooden spoon, scoop polenta onto 4 dinner plates. Sprinkle crumbled Gorgonzola cheese on each serving or serve separately.

All'Italiana: Enjoy this dish with

an Orvieto Classico or Pinot

Grigio wine.

Per Serving:
Calories: 186   Total Fat: 8 g   Sat. Fat: 5 g   Chol.: 21 mg

Baked Polenta with Ricotta

Polenta Pasticciata con Ricotta

Serves: 6
Preparation Time: 45 minutes
Cooking Time: 30 minutes

2 quarts water
1 teaspoon salt
2 cups purchased precooked
polenta or cooked Basic
Polenta (page (98)
15 ounces skim-milk ricotta
cheese
Salt and pepper to taste
1/4 cup freshly grated Parmesan
cheese
1 tablespoon margarine

This classic dish is easy to prepare and guaranteed to make polenta a frequent choice at dinner time, especially on cold nights when you desire a satisfying hot meal.

In a large pan, bring water and salt to a boil. Stir in polenta. When polenta has absorbed water, pour out on a damp, clean, flat surface such as a foil-lined countertop or baking sheet or a wooden board. Spray a rolling pin with nonstick cooking spray to keep polenta from sticking. Roll polenta out until 1/2 inch thick. Let cool. Preheat oven to 375F (190C). In a large bowl, combine ricotta cheese, salt and pepper until smooth. Spray a nonstick baking dish (3 to 4 inches deep) with nonstick cooking spray. Cut polenta into strips to fit baking dish. Line bottom of prepared baking dish with one layer of polenta. Spread a 1/4-inch layer of ricotta cheese over polenta, and sprinkle with 1 tablespoon Parmesan cheese. Continue layers until all polenta and ricotta cheese have been used, ending with polenta. Dot with margarine and sprinkle with the remaining Parmesan cheese. Bake 30 minutes, or until top is golden-brown.

All'Italiana: I enjoy this dish most with a chilled glass of Barbera or Sotturguro wine.

Per Serving:
Calories: 294   Total Fat: 9 g   Sat. Fat: 5 g   Chol.: 25 mg

Rice with Mushrooms

Risotto con Funghi

Serves: 8
Preparation Time: 10 minutes
Cooking Time: 25 minutes

3 cups water
1-1/2 cups dried porcini
   mushrooms
1 medium-size onion, coarsely
   chopped
2 garlic cloves, crushed
2 cups arborio or short-grain
   white rice
1-3/4 cups chicken broth
1/4 teaspoon salt
1/4 teaspoon pepper
2 tablespoons margarine
1/4 cup grated Parmesan
   cheese

This dish utilizes one of the North's best loved native delicacies—mushrooms! Former ambassador to the United Kingdom, Drew Dudley requested this dish at every dinner I catered for him.

Bring water to a boil in a small pan, then remove from heat and add mushrooms. Let soak 15 minutes—do not drain. Spray a large nonstick pan with nonstick cooking spray. Add onion, garlic and rice and cook over medium heat 3 to 5 minutes, or until ingredients are golden. Reduce heat and add chicken broth, salt, pepper and mushrooms plus soaking water. Cover and cook 11 minutes, or until rice is tender. Remove from heat and let stand 5 to 7 minutes. Stir in margarine and Parmesan cheese. Pour onto dinner plates.

Variations: If dried porcini mushrooms are hard to find, easier-to-find shiitake mushrooms can be substituted. My daughter Emily is a vegetarian and will not cook with chicken broth, but she makes this, and other delicious dishes, requiring chicken broth, with vegetable broth instead.

All'Italiana: For the total effect, serve risotto with a ring of tomato sauce around it. Purchased tomato pasta sauce will work fine or make your own, using the recipe on page 141.

Per Serving:
Calories: 238   *Total Fat: 3 g*   *Sat. Fat: 1 g*   *Chol.: 3 mg*

Milan-Style Rice

Risotto Milanese

Serves: 6
Preparation Time: 15 minutes
Cooking Time: 25 to 30 minutes

1 pinch of saffron
1 quart chicken broth
1 quart water
2 tablespoons olive oil
1-1/2 cups arborio or short-grain rice
1/4 teaspoon salt
1/2 cup grated Parmesan cheese (1-1/2 ounces)

No matter where you are, whenever you prepare this dish your heart will be under the stars of Milan. My class at the Culinary Institute of America loved this dish.

In a large pan, stir saffron into chicken broth and water. Let stand 10 minutes. Place pan over medium heat and bring to a boil. Reduce heat and simmer. In a medium-size pan over medium heat, heat oil. Add rice and salt and stir rapidly to prevent sticking. Cook rice about 3 minutes, or until coated with oil. Continue stirring and add simmering broth, 1 ladleful at a time. Cook rice, stirring, until liquid is absorbed before you add the next ladleful. Continue stirring and adding broth until risotto is sticky, yet creamy. This will take about 20 minutes. Stir in Parmesan cheese. Spoon into individual bowls or onto dinner plates and serve hot.

Variation: Instead of saffron, add 1 tablespoon tomato paste and 5 chopped basil leaves to chicken broth and water.

All'Italiana: To use leftover risotto, add enough egg whites or liquid egg substitute to make a spoonable consistency. Spoon into hot olive oil over medium heat. Cook 3 to 5 minutes, or until golden—for a delicious treat.

Per Serving:
Calories: 272   Total Fat: 8 g   Sat. Fat: 3 g   Chol.: 7 mg

Spiked Rice

Risotto alla Vodka

Serves: 6
Preparation Time: 10 minutes
Cooking Time: 30 minutes

1/2 teaspoon hot red pepper
  flakes
2 tablespoons vodka
2 quarts chicken broth
1 tablespoon margarine
2 cups arborio or short-grain
  rice
Salt to taste
1/4 cup Tofunetta (page 132)
2 to 4 tablespoons grated
  Parmesan cheese

Russia and Italy unite in gastronomic harmony in this combination using vodka, hot red pepper flakes and Parmesan cheese.

In a small bowl, add pepper to vodka. Set aside. In a medium-size pan over medium heat, bring chicken broth to a boil. Reduce heat and simmer. In another medium-size pan over medium heat, melt margarine. Add rice to margarine and stir rapidly to prevent sticking. Cook rice about 3 minutes, or until rice is coated with margarine. Continue stirring and add simmering broth, 1 ladleful at a time. Cook rice, stirring, until liquid is absorbed before you add the next ladleful. Continue stirring and adding broth until risotto is sticky, yet creamy. This will take about 20 minutes. Add salt to taste. Mix in Tofunetta and Parmesan cheese. Cook 3 to 5 minutes. Stir in vodka mixture. Mix well.

Variation: Substitute plain nonfat yogurt for Tofunetta.

All'Italiana: This tasty rice dish works best as an accent to grilled fish, chicken or beef.

Per Serving:
Calories: 346   Total Fat: 6g   Sat. Fat: 1 g   Chol.: 2 mg

Rice & Beans

Riso e Fagioli

Serves: 8
Preparation Time: 5 minutes
Cooking Time: 45 minutes

2 cups brown rice
2-1/2 cups water
1 (15-oz.) can black beans, drained
1 green bell pepper, coarsely chopped
1 red bell pepper, coarsely chopped
1 teaspoon garlic powder

Italy meets Mexico—two ancient cultures unite for a twist on an old favorite! I made this on many occasions for the Heinz family.

Preheat oven to 350F (175C). Cover and cook brown rice in water in a large pan over medium heat. Reduce heat if mixture begins to boil vigorously—rice should bubble gently. Check rice frequently, so that it does not stick to bottom of pan. Taste occasionally, and if rice is still crunchy as water disappears, add a bit more water, continue cooking and taste again. If rice is done before water is absorbed, uncover pan, increase heat and stir well until excess water evaporates. Remove from heat and set aside. Rinse beans with water through a colander. Transfer beans and rice into large baking dish. Stir in bell peppers and garlic powder. Bake 10 minutes, or until hot.

Variation: Use 1 cup dried black beans instead of canned beans. Follow package directions regarding soaking and cooking times.

All'Italiana: Sprinkle with 1/2 cup shredded skim-milk mozzarella or, for a Mexican touch, low-fat, low-cholesterol Monterey jack cheese before baking.

Per Serving:
Calories: 201   Total Fat: 2 g   Sat. Fat: 0.4 g   Chol.: 0 mg

Rice with Pumpkin

Riso e Zucca

Serves: 4
Preparation Time: 15 minutes
Cooking Time: 20 minutes

1 tablespoon olive oil
1 small onion (optional),
  chopped
1 cup short-grain rice
2 cups chicken broth
2 cups chopped fresh pumpkin

At dinner time sharp, the rice will turn into pumpkin. This is one of my favorites!

In a large pan over low heat, heat olive oil. Add onion, if using, and sauté until it is translucent. Add rice and stir until rice is covered with oil. Add chicken broth. Cook 5 to 6 minutes and add pumpkin. Bring to a boil. Reduce heat, cover and simmer 10 to 11 minutes, or until rice is tender. Let stand 5 minutes and serve.

Variation: When pumpkin is not in season, prepare this dish with the same amount of fresh acorn squash or summer squash.

All'Italiana: This gorgeous dish is a perfect accompaniment to a grilled white fish. The white and bright yellow make a beautiful combination.

Per Serving:
Calories: 233   Total Fat: 4 g   Sat. Fat: 0.8 g   Chol.: 0 mg

Baked Rice

Risotto al Forno

Serves: 8
Preparation Time: 15 minutes
Cooking Time: 40 minutes

2 tablespoons olive oil
1 small onion, coarsely chopped
2 cups arborio or short-grain rice
7 chopped fresh basil leaves
2 cups chicken broth
2 cups water
1/2 cup dried porcini mushrooms
1-1/2 teaspoons salt
3 tablespoons grated Parmesan cheese
2 tablespoons margarine

The unexpected tastes divine! Fresh basil and dried porcini mushrooms add subtle flavors.

Preheat oven to 375F (190C). In a large nonstick pan over medium heat, heat olive oil. Add onion and cook 5 minutes, or until onion is translucent. Add rice and stir until rice is coated with oil. Remove from heat. Stir in basil, chicken broth, water, mushrooms and salt. Mix gently. Return to heat and bring to a boil. Transfer into a nonstick baking dish. Cover and bake 25 minutes. Stir in Parmesan cheese and margarine. Spoon onto dinner plates and serve.

Variations: Chicken bouillon and even vegetable bouillon work very well in this recipe. However, beef or fish bouillon won't work so well. Also, 1/2 tablespoon dried basil can be substituted for fresh basil.

All'Italiana: This dish can stand on its own or as a complement to grilled beef, lamb or game.

Per Serving:
Calories: 235   Total Fat: 6 g   Sat. Fat: 1 g   Chol.: 2 mg

Focaccie, Gnocchi, Pane e Pisarei

Italian Breads & Dumplings

The traditional meets the trendy. Recipes featured in this section enjoy the distinction of being crossovers from old-fashioned Northern Italian fare to popular items of today. I hope my recipes will become more than a passing trend in your home.

Focaccia is a fine example of a traditional Italian dish that has recently become popular in America. Focaccia, or pizette, has always been a common afternoon snack in Italy, but it has taken a long time to catch on in America. Although focaccia is now available ready-made for American cooks to top with their favorite items, I hope my simple recipes for focaccia will persuade you to make the real thing at home.

Up until now, gnocchi and pisarei have not really enjoyed the popularity of focaccia or pasta, but these traditional dishes account for a sizable portion of the Northern Italian diet. As versatile as pasta and as easy to prepare, gnocchi and pisarei are destined to become frequent products of your kitchen. Follow my recipes and you'll see what you've been missing!

Focaccia with Garlic & Onions

Focaccia Aglio e Cipolla

Serves: 8
Preparation Time: 2-1/2 hours including soaking and rising times
Cooking Time: About 25 minutes

2 medium-size onions
2 garlic cloves
1 cup hot water
1 (1/4-oz.) package fast-rise yeast
1 teaspoon sugar
3 to 3-1/4 cups all-purpose flour
6 tablespoons olive oil
1 teaspoon coarse salt
1/2 teaspoon freshly ground pepper
1 tablespoon dried rosemary (optional)

All'Italiana: The basic recipe for focaccia is a playground for Italian tastes. Top with vegetables, cheese or anything that strikes your fancy.

As you make this more and more you will know exactly how much garlic, onions and salt you like on your focaccia. My daughter Monica always puts much less than I do.

Coarsely chop onions and garlic. Let soak 1 hour in hot water in a medium-size bowl. Strain, but reserve water. Reheat water to lukewarm. Add yeast and sugar to water in a medium-size bowl and let stand 10 minutes until foamy. Add flour and 2 tablespoons of the olive oil to yeast mixture. Mix until it forms a soft dough. Roll out dough with an oiled rolling pin to a long oval shape. Spray a non-stick 15″ x 12″ baking pan or traditional 12-inch round pizza pan with nonstick cooking spray. Place dough in pan and gently stretch almost to edges of pan. Cover with a clean towel and let rise in a warm place 1 hour. When dough is risen, dip your fingers in remaining olive oil and gradually shape the dough to fill the pan. Work slowly, continually dipping your fingers in the oil and shaping dough until all the oil has been used. Cover, set aside and let rise 30 minutes. Preheat oven to 425F (220C) 15 minutes before dough has finished rising. Arrange onions and garlic on top of dough and sprinkle with coarse salt and pepper to taste. Sprinkle with rosemary, if using. Bake 25 to 30 minutes. To check for doneness lift focaccia up with a spatula—the bottom should be golden-brown.

Per Serving:
Calories: 293   Total Fat: 11 g   Sat. Fat: 2 g   Chol.: 0 mg

Focaccia with Olive Oil & Salt

Focaccia Olio e Sale

Serves: 6
Preparation Time: 1-1/2 hours including rising time
Cooking Time: 20 to 25 minutes

- 3/4 cup warm water (110F, 45C)
- 1 (1/4-oz.) package fast-rise yeast
- 1/4 teaspoon sugar
- 2-1/2 cups all-purpose flour
- 1/4 cup olive oil
- 4 tablespoons coarse kosher salt

Italy's answer to the pretzel!

Pour water into a large bowl, then add yeast and sugar. Let stand 10 minutes until foamy. Add flour and mix well to form a soft dough. Turn dough out onto a lightly floured surface and knead gently. Roll out dough with an oiled rolling pin to a long oval shape. Spray a nonstick 15" x 12" baking pan or 12-inch pizza pan with nonstick cooking spray. Place dough in pan and gently stretch dough almost to edges of pan. Cover with a clean towel and let rise in a warm place 1 hour. When dough is risen, dip your fingers in olive oil and gradually shape the dough to fill the pan. Work slowly, continually dipping your fingers in the olive oil and shaping the dough until all the olive oil has been used, then set aside and let rise 30 minutes. Preheat oven to 375F (190C) 15 minutes before dough has finished rising. Sprinkle with salt and bake 20 to 25 minutes. To check for doneness lift focaccia up with a spatula—the bottom should be golden-brown.

Variation: Use whole-wheat flour instead of white for a truly health-oriented treat.

All'Italiana: One Italian custom I miss is the *Passagiata,* which literally means "stroll." Late in the afternoon, especially in coastal towns, Italians stroll about town, savor cappucini in cafés or munch on focaccie.

Per Serving:
Calories: 270   Total Fat: 10 g   Sat. Fat: 1 g   Chol.: 0 mg

Garden Bread

Pane di Verdura

Serves: 8
Preparation Time: 10 minutes
Cooking Time: 75 minutes

4 (10-oz.) packages frozen
   chopped spinach
1 cup liquid egg substitute
2 tablespoons margarine
1 tablespoon all-purpose flour
1/2 cup skim milk
1 teaspoon salt
1 teaspoon pepper
Pinch of nutmeg

This is a testament to the Florentine region's clever use of spinach. Perfect for a garden party.

Preheat oven to 325F (165C). Spray a soufflé mold or deep bread pan with nonstick cooking spray. Cook frozen spinach according to package directions. Drain and squeeze excess water from spinach with your hands and transfer to a large bowl. Add egg substitute and mix well. Set aside. In a small pan over medium heat, melt margarine. Slowly stir in flour. Cook 2 minutes. Stir in skim milk and cook 1 minute. Add to spinach mixture. Stir in salt, pepper and nutmeg. Pour mixture into prepared soufflé mold or bread pan. Place pan in a large, deep pan. Add enough water to come up 1/3 of the side of the pan. Bake 1 hour or until a knife inserted in center comes out clean. Unmold or serve from pan.

Variation: Substitute 5 cups fresh spinach for frozen spinach. Cook in a little water over medium heat 5 to 10 minutes, or until tender.

All'Italiana: Especially popular in and around Florence where spinach is a staple in many recipes, this dish can be enjoyed instead of an omelet.

Per Serving:
Calories: 193   Total Fat: 8 g   Sat. Fat: 1 g   Chol.: 0 mg

Bread Dumplings, Piancentina Style

Pisarei e Faso alla Piancentina

Serves: 4
Preparation Time: 15 minutes
Cooking Time: 20

1-1/4 cups Classic Tomato Sauce (page 141) or purchased tomato pasta sauce

1 (15-oz.) can or 2 cups cooked pinto beans, drained

3/4 cup water

1 cup chopped Italian bread

2 cups all-purpose flour

1/4 teaspoon salt

This is Italian "comfort" food. With every bite, the blues will fade away.

Heat tomato sauce and add pinto beans to hot sauce. Keep warm over low heat in a covered pan. In a medium-size pan over high heat, bring the water to a boil. Add bread to a large bowl. Pour 1/4 cup boiling water over bread. With your hands, mix together. Add flour salt and continue adding water until mixture becomes a soft dough. You may not need all of the remaining water. Turn out dough and knead on a lightly floured surface. Knead 1 minute, or until dough is solid, yet soft, like pizza dough. Break dough into 4 balls. Roll each ball into a 1/2-inch-thick strip. With a sharp knife, cut each strip into 1/2-inch-long logs. Pour 2 cups water into a large pan and bring to a boil over high heat. When water boils, drop dumplings into water. Cook 2 to 3 minutes, or until dumplings float to the top. Remove as they float with a slotted spoon or spatula. Divide among plates and pour warm sauce over each portion.

Variation: This recipe was my sister Mafalda's favorite when we were kids. She still prepares it to this day, but she forgoes the knife and breaks and rolls the pisarei by hand.

All'Italiana: A typical Italian peasant dish and substantial meal loaded with protein and carbohydrates, we ate a lot of this while I was growing up.

Per Serving:
Calories: 374   Total Fat: 1 g   Sat. Fat: 0.2 g   Chol.: 0 mg

Spinach Dumplings I

Gnocchi Verdi I

Serves: 4
Preparation Time: 30 minutes
plus overnight refrigeration
Cooking Time: 25 to 30
minutes

2 (10-oz.) packages frozen
    chopped spinach
6 egg whites
1/4 teaspoon salt
15 ounces part-skim ricotta
    cheese
1 cup farmer cheese
4 tablespoons grated Parmesan
    cheese
1/2 cup all-purpose flour, sifted
2 pinches nutmeg
1/4 teaspoon pepper
2 to 4 tablespoons margarine

*This is one way many Italian mamas get their
bambini to eat their spinach.*

Cook frozen spinach according to package directions.
Drain excess water from spinach and let cool. Taking 3
tablespoons of spinach in your hand at a time, squeeze
gently to remove all liquid. Place squeezed spinach onto a
plate and set aside. In a large bowl, whip egg whites vigorously with a whisk 2 minutes, until frothy. With a fork,
stir in spinach, salt, ricotta cheese, farmer cheese and 3
tablespoons of the Parmesan cheese until blended. Add
flour, 1 pinch of nutmeg and pepper. With your hands,
work ingredients until they are well blended. Refrigerate
overnight, or at least 6 to 8 hours. When ready to cook,
preheat oven to 450F (230C). In a large pan, bring 4 cups
salted water to a boil. Spray a shallow nonstick baking dish
with nonstick cooking spray. Sprinkle a work surface with
flour. Spoon out spinach mixture with a tablespoon and,
using your hands, roll into little balls (gnocchi) along
floured surface. Drop gnocchi into pot, one at a time. As
gnocchi begin to rise to the surface, which should be in 3
to 5 minutes, remove them with a slotted spoon. Drain off
water and arrange neatly in prepared baking dish, so that
gnocchi are touching lightly but not overlapping. In a
small pan over medium heat, melt margarine. Drizzle melted margarine over gnocchi. Sprinkle with the remaining
Parmesan cheese and a pinch of nutmeg. Bake 7 minutes,
until lightly browned.

Variation: Substitute 2-1/2 cups fresh spinach for frozen
spinach. Cook in enough water to cover over medium heat
5 to 10 minutes, or until tender.

All'Italiana: Northern Italians

love gnocchi with meat sauce.

Try it with Turkey Meatballs

(page 54), on the side.

Per Serving:
Calories: 420   Total Fat: 18 g   Sat. Fat: 8 g   Chol.: 42 mg

Spinach Dumplings II

Gnocchi Verdi II

Serves: 4
Preparation Time: 20 minutes
plus 2 hours refrigeration
Cooking Time: 30 minutes

2 (10-oz.) packages frozen
   chopped spinach
15 ounces part-skim ricotta
   cheese
4 tablespoons grated Parmesan
   cheese
5 tablespoons sifted all-
   purpose flour
3 egg whites
Pinch of nutmeg
Pinch of salt
2 tablespoons all-purpose flour
1 cup nonfat plain yogurt
1 tablespoon margarine

When my daughter Emily was growing up, this was her favorite. She thought it was such a treat, she'd even eat cold leftovers for breakfast the next morning!

Cook frozen spinach according to package directions. Drain all excess water from cooked spinach. In a large bowl, combine spinach, ricotta cheese, 3 tablespoons of the Parmesan cheese, the 5 tablespoons flour, egg whites, nutmeg and salt. Refrigerate 2 hours. In a large pan, bring 2 quarts salted water to a boil. Sprinkle a work surface with flour. Spoon out spinach mixture with a tablespoon and, using your hands, roll into little balls (gnocchi) along floured surface. Drop gnocchi into pot, one at a time. As gnocchi begin to rise to the surface, remove them with a slotted spoon. Drain off water. Preheat broiler. Spray a shallow baking dish with nonstick cooking spray. Spread half of yogurt in prepared dish and arrange gnocchi so that gnocchi are touching lightly but not overlapping. Pour remaining yogurt over gnocchi, dot with margarine and sprinkle with the remaining Parmesan cheese. Broil 5 to 7 minutes, or until top of gnocchi is crispy.

All'Italiana: Gnocchi works well as a change from pasta as a first course. Serve this with a fine Orvieto or Pinot Grigio.

Per Serving:
Calories: 294   Total Fat: 12 g   Sat. Fat: 6 g   Chol.: 37 mg

Pumpkin Bread

Pane Zucca

Serves: 6
Preparation Time: 20 minutes plus 1-1/2 hours rising time
Cooking Time: 45 minutes

1/2 cup warm water (110F, 45C)
1 (1/4-oz.) package fast-rise yeast
Pinch of sugar
2-1/2 cups plus 1/2 tablespoon all-purpose flour
1 cup pumpkin puree (canned or cooked)
1/2 teaspoon salt
Pinch of ground nutmeg
Pinch of ground cloves
3 tablespoons cornmeal

This bread looks dangerous. Its looks say butter and eggs, but in reality it is the pumpkin that gives this tasty bread its glorious color.

Pour water into a large bowl, then add yeast and sugar. Let stand 10 minutes until foamy. Add the 2-1/2 cups flour, pumpkin, salt, nutmeg and cloves. Stir with a large spoon until ingredients form a dough. Turn out dough onto a lightly floured surface. Knead dough until soft and silky, dusting with flour if needed. Spray a large nonstick baking sheet with nonstick cooking spray. Place dough ball onto baking sheet, cover with a clean towel and let rise in a warm place 1 hour, or until doubled in size. About 15 minutes before dough has finished rising, preheat oven to 450F (230C). Form dough into a long, wide loaf shape. Picture in your mind a purchased loaf of Italian bread when shaping the dough. Sprinkle cornmeal evenly onto baking sheet. Dust loaf with the 1/2 tablespoon flour and arrange on cornmeal. Reduce heat to 375F (190C) and bake 45 to 60 minutes, or until golden-brown.

Variation: To make Panini Zucca: Follow the same directions as for Pane Zucca but after letting dough rise once, use a rolling pin and flatten dough to about 1 inch thick. Cover and let rise 1 hour more. About 20 minutes before dough has finished rising, preheat oven to 500F (260C). With a round cookie cutter, cut out dough into circles—these are your panini (little bread). Place panini onto a baking sheet. Turn off oven. Place panini in oven and bake 10 minutes or until golden-brown. The shut-off oven will bake the panini nicely.

All'Italiana: My sister Mafalda loved this bread. It's sweet and best eaten warm and fresh from the oven with a pat of margarine.

Per Serving:
Calories: 217   Total Fat: 0.9 g   Sat. Fat: 0.5 g   Chol.: 0 mg

Verdure

Vegetables

When Italian flair touches vegetables they become more than just side dishes—they become stand-out meals in their own right. Wake up the true personality of vegetables and discover simple ways to dress them up. Look again at many long-ignored ones like escarole, asparagus and rutabaga.

Sedani Brasati (page 121), Fagioli Nostrani (page 123), Melanzane Farcite al Gorgonzola (page 124) and Scarola e Pomodori Amalfitana (page 127) are just a few examples of dishes which make vegetables very Italian and *molto, molto delizioso!* Each recipe is simple to make and you'll see that once you try them, plain boiled vegetables just won't do anymore.

Carrot Puree

Puré di Carote

Serves: 6
Preparation Time: 10 minutes
Cooking Time: 25 minutes

1 bunch carrots
1 medium-size potato
1/2 cup Tofunetta (page 132)

Most often, adults have to bribe kids to eat vegetables like broccoli, turnips and rutabaga. But when covered in this sweet puree, these vegetables become enticing even to children.

Peel and cut carrots and potato into quarters. In a large pot over medium heat, boil carrots and potato in enough water to cover about 20 minutes, or until tender. Saving 1 cup of cooking water, drain carrots and potato through a colander. Put carrots and potato back into pot and add Tofunetta. Simmer over medium heat 5 minutes. In a food processor equipped with the metal blade, process 15 to 20 seconds. Serve as a side dish. To make into a sauce, add a little of the reserved water until puree reaches a thick smooth consistency. Serve over boiled or steamed broccoli, turnips or rutabaga.

Variation: Substitute 1 cup plain nonfat yogurt for Tofunetta. However, the flavor will not be quite as good.

All'Italiana: Mashed potatoes aren't a staple in Italy, but pureed vegetables take their place as a favorite of kids. My daughter Monica prepares this as a meal for her little girl, Clara.

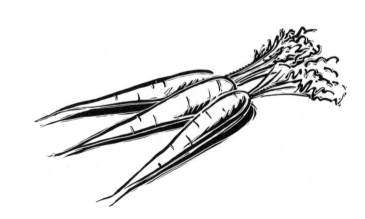

Per Serving:
Calories: 62   Total Fat: 0.6 g   Sat. Fat: 0 g   Chol.: 0 mg

120

Braised Celery

Sedani Brasati

Serves: 4
Preparation Time: 5 minutes
Cooking Time: 20 to 30 minutes

2 celery bunches
2 tablespoons olive oil
1 teaspoon sugar
1/4 cup water

A tradition in Italian farm country, braised celery can be a healthy, hearty addition to a family dinner or an elegant selection at a formal affair.

Remove darker, outer stalks of celery until you reach the light green, leafy heart. Cut off leaves and discard. Save outside stalks for another use. Cut hearts of celery lengthwise into quarters. In a large nonstick pan over medium heat, brown hearts of celery in olive oil and sugar. When brown on all sides, add water. Reduce heat and cover. Simmer 20 to 30 minutes, or until tender, checking frequently. If water evaporates, add a little more water as needed, to keep celery moist and from burning. Remove from pan and arrange on a platter for a formal dinner, or on dinner plates at a casual meal.

Variations: Use 1 tablespoon brown sugar instead of granulated sugar. Try this recipe with 5 heads of Belgian endive cut into halves instead of celery. It is another terrific dish!

All'Italiana: My mother made this for us frequently, but she did not add the sugar—a French touch that gives this simple peasant dish panache.

Per Serving:
Calories: 76   Total Fat: 7 g   Sat. Fat: 1 g   Chol.: 0 mg

Tomatoes Stuffed with Italian Salmon Salad

Pomodoro Farciti con Orzo e Salmone

Serves: 6
Preparation Time: 20 minutes plus 1 hour refrigeration time
Cooking Time: 5 to 10 minutes

3/4 cup uncooked orzo pasta
2 garlic cloves
1 cup basil leaves
1 tablespoon olive oil
1 teaspoon Dijon-style mustard
1 (6-1/8-oz.) can pink salmon, drained
6 medium-size ripe tomatoes
Salt and pepper to taste

Clients love this at summer parties where the living is easy and all they want is something light to nibble on.

Cook orzo according to package directions until al dente. Drain and set aside. In a blender set to medium speed or a small food processor equipped with the metal blade, process garlic, basil leaves, olive oil and mustard 10 seconds. In a large bowl, combine cooked orzo and garlic mixture. Gently mix in salmon. Cut tops off tomatoes and scoop out seeds. Discard both tops and seeds. Season salmon mixture with salt and pepper. Fill tomatoes with mixture. Cover and refrigerate at least 1 hour. Serve chilled.

All'Italiana: Delicious on its own for a light summer lunch Enjoy it with a chilled white wine.

Per Serving:
Calories: 140   Total Fat: 5 g   Sat. Fat: 1 g   Chol.: 16 mg

Black-Eyed Peas

Fagioli Nostrani

Serves: 6
Preparation Time: 15 minutes
Cooking Time: About 25 minutes

3 cups black-eyed peas
   (frozen, fresh or canned)
1 tablespoon olive oil
20 basil leaves
2 garlic cloves, chopped
1 small onion, chopped
1 medium-size carrot, chopped
1 tablespoon red wine vinegar
Salt and pepper to taste

A favorite of America's South gets a lesson in flavor from the north of Italy! This was a favorite of the hired hands who worked the fields.

Cook frozen black-eyed peas according to package directions. If using fresh, cook in 2 cups water over medium heat 15 to 20 minutes, or until tender. If using canned black-eyed peas, rinse with water in a colander. Place black-eyed peas in a medium-size serving bowl. Set aside. In a medium-size nonstick skillet over medium heat, heat olive oil. Add basil, garlic, onion and carrot and sauté 5 minutes. Stir in vinegar. Cook 1 minute. Combine with black-eyed peas. Season with salt and pepper and serve.

Variation: My daughter Emily substitutes white beans for black-eyed peas. Sometimes she adds 3/4 cup albacore tuna to the mixture and serves it over pasta for a quick-fix, nutritional meal.

All'Italiana: Try these black-eyed peas over white rice or pasta for a main dish.

Per Serving:
Calories: 146   Total Fat: 3 g   Sat. Fat: 0.5 g   Chol.: 0 mg

Baked Eggplant with Gorgonzola

Melanzane Farcite al Gorgonzola

Serves: 6
Preparation Time: 10 minutes
Cooking Time: 20 minutes

2 small Italian eggplants
1/4 teaspoon salt
1/4 teaspoon pepper
2 tablespoons all-purpose flour
2 tablespoons olive oil
1/2 cup crumbled Gorgonzola
    cheese (2 ounces)
2 cups chopped fresh tomatoes
10 basil leaves, chopped
15 anchovy fillets (optional)
2 tablespoons grated Parmesan
    cheese

When I prepared this at the Long Island estate of William S. Paley, founder of CBS, I added anchovy fillets to the Gorgonzola filling and served baked ziti as a complementary dish.

Cut unpeeled eggplant lengthwise into 1/4-inch-thick slices. Combine salt, pepper and flour on a large plate. Roll eggplant slices in flour mixture until coated. In a large nonstick skillet over medium heat, heat olive oil. Add eggplant slices and sauté 3 minutes on each side, or until golden. Remove from heat with a slotted spoon or spatula and lay on paper towels to drain. Preheat oven to 425F (220C). Spray a shallow baking dish with nonstick cooking spray. Arrange one layer of eggplant in prepared dish. Sprinkle Gorgonzola cheese, tomatoes and basil over eggplant. Top with anchovy fillets, if using. Arrange remaining eggplant on top of Gorgonzola cheese mixture. Sprinkle with Parmesan cheese. Bake 5 minutes, or until bubbly.

All'Italiana: Italians will add other flavors such as roasted peppers to the Gorgonzola cheese mixture. Make this dish once and you'll know which ingredients to add to make your own distinct creation.

Per Serving:
Calories: 130   Total Fat: 0.8 g   Sat. Fat: 3 g   Chol.: 10 mg

Braised Escarole

Scarola Stufata

Serves: 4
Preparation Time: 10 minutes
Cooking Time: 13 to 18 minutes

1 bunch escarole
3 tablespoons olive oil
1 garlic clove, minced

Escarole is a vegetable so many people ignore, quite possibly because they don't know what to do with it. Well, here is a recipe that is sure to make it a permanent fixture on your grocery list.

Separate escarole leaves. Rinse well and drain, yet leave it somewhat damp. In a large pan over medium-low heat, heat olive oil. Add garlic and sauté 3 minutes. Do not brown garlic. Add escarole. Reduce heat and cover. Turn escarole occasionally, flipping it over with a spatula so that every side will soak up garlic and olive oil. Simmer 10 to 15 minutes, or until escarole is tender.

Variation: This dish works with broccoli, too!

All'Italiana: Braised Escarole complements chicken perfectly, especially sautéed chicken breasts.

Per Serving:
Calories: 132   Total Fat: 11 g   Sat. Fat: 2 g   Chol.: 0 mg

Rosemary Potatoes

Patate alla Rosemarino

Serves: 6
Preparation Time: 10
Cooking Time: 70 minutes

5 russet potatoes
2 tablespoons margarine
2 tablespoons olive oil
1 teaspoon dried or fresh
 rosemary
1 garlic clove, minced

There is very little this dish will not complement. My favorite way to serve it is with a beautiful roasted chicken.

Preheat oven to 350F (175C). Peel potatoes, slice into thin rounds no thicker than 1/4 inch and place in a large bowl with enough water to cover. Once all potatoes have been peeled and cut, remove from water and dry thoroughly with paper towels. Set aside. In a large nonstick skillet over medium heat, heat margarine, olive oil, rosemary and garlic. Stir in potatoes and cook 5 minutes, or until golden-brown. Transfer potatoes into a large nonstick baking dish and arrange evenly. Bake 45 minutes, or until tender.

Variations: Instead of using 5 russet potatoes, use 10 small red potatoes which have been partially peeled. If desired, finish cooking potatoes on stovetop instead of in the oven. Cook about 10 minutes from the time potatoes turn golden-brown.

Hint: Grind the rosemary coarsely to release even more of its wonderful flavor.

All'Italiana: These potatoes make the perfect accent to all kinds of roasted meats.

Per Serving:
Calories: 156   Total Fat: 7 g   Sat. Fat: 1 g   Chol.: 0 mg

Escarole with Tomatoes

Scarola e Pomodori Amalfitana

Serves: 8
Preparation Time: 15 minutes
Cooking Time: 12 to 15 minutes

2 bunches escarole
4 medium-size ripe tomatoes
3 tablespoons olive oil
1/4 cup pine nuts
2 garlic cloves, sliced
9 anchovy fillets, minced
1 pinch each of salt and pepper

A light dish that will conjure up the image of a sunlit veranda overlooking the gentle waves of the Mediterranean.

Rinse and dry escarole. Tear into small pieces. Peel tomatoes, remove seeds and cut flesh into tiny pieces. Set aside. In a small pan over medium heat, heat 1 tablespoon of the olive oil. Add pine nuts and sauté 3 minutes, or until light brown on all sides. Remove from pan and drain on paper towels. In a large pan over medium heat, heat remaining olive oil. Add garlic and sauté 5 minutes, or until golden. With a fork, carefully remove garlic and discard. Reduce heat and add anchovy fillets. Cook 2 minutes or until anchovy fillets are soft. Stir in tomato pieces and escarole. Sprinkle with salt and pepper. Cook 3 to 5 minutes, or until escarole is tender. Transfer to a serving dish and sprinkle with toasted pine nuts.

All'Italiana: Be adventurous with Italian herbs. I prefer this dish with just salt and pepper, but feel free to experiment once you've prepared it a couple of times.

Per Serving:
Calories: 95   Total Fat: 9 g   Sat. Fat: 2 g   Chol.: 0 mg

Eggplant with Tomatoes

Melanzane al Pomodoro Torinesi

Serves: 4
Preparation Time: 15 minutes
plus 3 hours standing time
Cooking Time: 15 minutes

1 Italian eggplant
Salt
2 zucchini
1 medium-size onion, chopped
2 tomatoes
2 tablespoons olive oil
1 garlic clove, minced
5 basil leaves, chopped
Pinch each of salt, pepper and
    dried marjoram

A delicious blend of two distinctly Italian flavors.

Prepare vegetables well in advance, perhaps the morning of the meal. Peel eggplant, remove seeds and cut into bite-size pieces. Place in a colander and sprinkle with salt. Slice zucchini into thin rounds, sprinkle with salt and place in a small bowl. Peel and chop onion. Place in a small bowl, cover and set aside. Peel and chop tomatoes and put in another small bowl. Cover and set aside in a cool place. At least 3 hours later, in a large nonstick skillet over medium heat, heat olive oil. Add onion and stir. Pat eggplant with paper towels to remove any excess water. Add eggplant to skillet and combine with onion. Pat zucchini with paper towels, squeeze out excess water and add to skillet. Stir several times and add tomatoes. Cook 1 minute. Add garlic, basil and salt, pepper and marjoram. Reduce heat and simmer 5 minutes, or until vegetables are tender. Serve hot or cold.

All'Italiana: At a summer luncheon, serve this cold on a bed of Boston lettuce for a delicious meal, Turin style.

Per Serving:
Calories: 126   *Total Fat: 7 g*   *Sat. Fat: 1 g*   *Chol.: 0 mg*

128

Salse

Sauces & Garnishes

Forget heavy, cream-based sauces. The new sauces are made with vegetables, olive oil, yogurt or Tofunetta (page 132)—a skim milk and tofu combination which results in a delicious heavy cream substitute. I have collected regional favorites from Milan, Genoa, Piacenza and my hometown of Pitolo. Vegetables such as artichoke hearts, eggplant and radishes are dressed up in sauces and used as tasty garnishes. Regular mayonnaise is tossed aside, but its creamy texture and delicious flavor remain in alternatives that have less fat and no cholesterol. The sauces and garnishes listed here will be delicate accents to any dish and will never overpower with heavy textures or tastes. They will bring out the best in every dish you make.

Italy Does Tofu

Tofunetta

Yields: 1-1/2 cups
Preparation Time: 10 minutes
Cooking Time: 0

2/3 cup tofu
3/4 cup skim milk

Whatever heavy cream can do, Tofunetta can do too—but Tofunetta does it with low fat and low cholesterol. Soups made with it have the same velvety texture and creamy taste as if made with heavy cream.

In a blender set at high speed or a food processor equipped with the metal blade, process tofu and milk 1 minute or until creamy. For best results, Tofunetta should be made immediately before using.

All'Italiana: Try Tofunetta in soups, sauces and desserts.

Traditional Italian food enters the 90s!

Per 1/4 cup:
Calories: 32   Total Fat: 1 g   Sat. Fat: 0.3 g   Chol.: 0 mg

Simple Radish Garnish

Ravanelli Mezzi Cotti

Serves: 4
Preparation Time: 10 minutes
Cooking Time: 5 to 6 minutes

2 bunches radishes (about 2 to 3 cups)

Most people use radishes only in salads, never realizing what a beautiful accompaniment radishes can make to meat and fish. When cooked, radishes mellow in taste yet keep their brilliant color.

Wash and cut off stems and ends of radishes. Do not peel. In a medium-size pan, boil or steam radishes 5 to 6 minutes, or until radishes become soft. Serve whole or process in a food processor equipped with the metal blade until finely chopped. Spoon onto the side of meat or fish as a wonderful garnish that is as tasty as it is beautiful.

All'Italiana: Italians don't stop at just traditional uses of foods. This dish is a great example of the Italian talent for exposing a wider range of a vegetable's personality.

Per Serving:
Calories: 4   Total Fat: 0 g   Sat. Fat: 0 g   Chol.: 0 mg

Eggplant, Sicilian Style

Caponata alla Siciliana

Serves: 6
Preparation Time: 15 minutes plus 1 hour standing time
Cooking Time: 40 minutes to 1 hour

3 medium-size Italian eggplants
1 tablespoon salt
1/4 cup vegetable oil
3 medium-size onions, coarsely chopped
4 celery stalks, thinly sliced
2 garlic cloves, minced
35 ounces canned whole tomatoes
2 tablespoons red wine vinegar
1 tablespoon sugar
Salt and pepper to taste
12 pitted ripe olives, chopped
4 anchovy fillets, minced
2 tablespoons capers, drained
1/4 cup pine nuts (optional)
1/4 cup chopped pimientos (optional)

All'Italiana: Social Italians know that you can never be sure when a group of friends will stop by, so they keep delicacies, such as this dish, on hand for impromptu parties.

Pardon me as I stray south, but this is one of my favorite recipes and I want to share it with you. As much as Italy borrows from other nations, regions of Italy also influence one another a great deal.

Peel eggplant and cut into 1-1/2-inch cubes. Transfer eggplant into a bowl and sprinkle with salt. Let stand 50 minutes. Pat eggplant with paper towels and squeeze out excess water. In a medium-size pan over high heat, heat vegetable oil. Add a few eggplant pieces to hot oil at a time. Stir quickly, and as eggplant turns brown, add more eggplant until all is cooked. Set aside. Spray a large nonstick pan with nonstick cooking spray. Add onions and cook over medium heat 5 minutes, or until translucent. Add celery and garlic and cook 5 minutes. Add tomatoes, wine vinegar and sugar to the onion mixture. With a spoon or fork, gently break up the tomatoes until they make a chunky, thick sauce. Add salt and pepper to taste. Bring to a boil, reduce heat and cover. Cook 5 minutes. Add olives. Cook 3 minutes. Add eggplant and bring to a boil. Reduce heat and cook 5 more minutes. Add anchovy fillets and capers and, if using, pine nuts and/or pimientos. Cook 5 minutes, or until anchovy fillets are hot and soft. Pour over steaming pasta or refrigerate and serve cold as an appetizer.

Hint: This will keep in the refrigerator several days if tightly covered.

Per Serving:
Calories: 204   Total Fat: 12 g   Sat. Fat:1   Chol.: 2 mg

Special Milanese Sauce

Gremolata

Serves: 2
Preparation Time: 10 minutes
Cooking Time: 0

3 tablespoons grated lemon
    peel
3 tablespoons coarsely
    chopped parsley
10 anchovy fillets packed in oil
1 tablespoon of oil from
    anchovy fillets

As much a fixture in Milan as temperamental opera stars and lords of fashion, this sauce adds a popular accent to meat.

In a small food processor equipped with the metal blade, process all ingredients 10 seconds, or by hand with a knife, chop ingredients until they form a thick, smooth paste.

All'Italiana: The Milanese accent braised or boiled beef, lamb and even white fish, with this tangy, pungent sauce. They love dramatic flair as much in their cooking as they do in their lives!

Per Serving:
Calories: 104   Total Fat: 8 g   Sat. Fat: 1 g   Chol.: 17 mg

Artichokes Braised in Oil

Carciofi Sotto Olio

Serves: 4
Preparation Time: 5 minutes
plus 1 hour refrigeration
Cooking Time: 12 minutes

1 (10-oz.) package frozen
   artichoke hearts, thawed
2 tablespoons apple cider
   vinegar
1/2 cup olive oil
1 garlic clove, minced
1 teaspoon hot red pepper
   flakes
Salt and black pepper to taste

Great when made in advance, the host can take this out of the freezer and serve as a garnish or a complement to many meat, fish or poultry dishes.

In a medium-size pan over medium heat, cook artichoke hearts in vinegar 5 minutes. Add olive oil, garlic and pepper flakes, salt and pepper. Bring to a boil and cook 6 to 7 minutes. Remove from heat, transfer to a serving bowl and let cool. Refrigerate 1 hour before serving or freeze, tightly sealed, up to 1 week for later use.

All'Italiana: As well as it goes with braised lamb or beef, this dish is also terrific on its own on a thick slice of Italian bread.

Per Serving:
Calories: 277   Total Fat: 27 g   Sat. Fat: 4 g   Chol.: 0 mg

Red Mayonnaise

Maionese Rossa

Serves: 8
Preparation Time: 15 minutes
Cooking Time: 0

2 tablespoons coarsely
   chopped red bell pepper
1 tablespoon Dijon-style
   mustard
1 garlic clove, crushed
1/4 cup liquid egg substitute
1 cup corn oil
Pinch of salt
Pinch of black pepper
1 tablespoon white wine
   vinegar

Dressing to thrill!

In a blender or a food processor equipped with the metal blade, combine bell pepper, mustard, garlic and egg substitute until smooth. Add corn oil a little at a time, continuing to process, until mayonnaise is thick and creamy. Add salt, pepper and vinegar and process 30 seconds. Mayonnaise should be thick and creamy. Serve in a small bowl.

All'Italiana: This sauce is served in Italy as an accompaniment to meat or as a sauce over asparagus and artichokes.

Per Serving:
Calories: 250   Total Fat: 28 g   Sat. Fat: 4 g   Chol.: 0 mg

Green Sauce, Piancentine Style

Salsa Verde Piancentina

Serves: 6
Preparation Time: 10 minutes
Cooking Time: 0

1 large bunch parsley, large
   stems removed
4 garlic cloves
1 cup chopped Italian bread
   (without crust)
1/2 cup olive oil
1 tablespoon vinegar
Salt and pepper to taste

Toss out that jar of mayonnaise. Here's a quickie sauce that's great news for leftover meats and terrific news for your health.

In a mortar or a food processor equipped with the metal blade, process all ingredients until very finely chopped. Serve as an accompaniment to cold meats, especially lean roast beef or leftover leg of lamb.

All'Italiana: This is a favorite sauce throughout the Emilia-Romagna Province to serve over cold meats.

Per Serving:
Calories: 194   *Total Fat: 18 g*   *Sat. Fat: 3 g*   *Chol.: 0 mg*

Dill Mayonnaise

Maionese al Anèto

Serves: 6
Preparation Time: 15 minutes plus refrigeration time
Cooking Time: 0

1 cup dill leaves
1 tablespoon Dijon-style mustard
1/4 cup liquid egg substitute
1 cup corn oil
1 /4 teaspoon salt
1/4 teaspoon pepper
1/4 teaspoon white vinegar

Toss that fatty mayonnaise aside and make a more flavorful alternative to those "light" products. Use it with fish and cold meats for a healthier dip.

In a blender or a food processor equipped with the metal blade, finely chop dill. Leave dill in blender or food processor. Add mustard and egg substitute. Process 30 seconds, or until thickened. Add corn oil a little at a time and continue processing. Add salt, pepper and vinegar. Process 30 seconds, or until mayonnaise is thick and creamy. Refrigerate 1/2 to 1 hour. Serve chilled with hot or cold meat or fish.

Variation: About 1/4 cup dried dill can be substituted for fresh dill.

All'Italiana: Make a great Italian sandwich—spread this mayonnaise on Italian bread and cover with fresh tomatoes, mozzarella cheese, grilled peppers and eggplant. *Abbondanza!*

Per Serving:
Calories: 338   Total Fat: 37 g   Sat. Fat: 5 g   Chol.: 0 mg

Genoa Pesto Sauce

Il Vero Pesto alla Genovese

Serves: 8
Preparation Time: 3 minutes
Cooking Time: 0

3 cups basil leaves
1 garlic clove
3 tablespoons pine nuts
1/2 cup grated Parmesan
   cheese (1-1/2 ounces)
2 tablespoons grated Romano
   cheese
3/4 cup olive oil
Salt to taste

The Genoese are as distinct as the sauce they made famous. Just like the people of Genoa, pesto is memorable, full of taste and great to have at a dinner party.

In a mortar, or a food processor equipped with metal blade, process basil, garlic and pine nuts 30 seconds, or until they form a paste. Transfer ingredients to a medium-size bowl. Stir in cheeses. Slowly stir in olive oil until all ingredients combine to form a thick paste. Stop adding olive oil, even if it is less than the recipe calls for, as soon as the ingredients form a thick paste—the sauce should not be runny. Stir in salt.

All'Italiana: Cook pasta al

dente. As you drain pasta,

reserve 1/2 cup cooking water.

In the same pot you cooked

pasta in, combine pasta and

pesto. If needed, stir in a little

reserved water.

Per Serving:
Calories: 240   Total Fat: 24 g   Sat. Fat: 4 g   Chol.: 7 mg

Classic Tomato Sauce

Salsa di Pomodoro

Serves: 6
Preparation Time: 10 minutes
Cooking Time: 30 minutes

4 large ripe tomatoes
1 tablespoon olive oil
1 small onion, coarsely
  chopped
1 garlic clove, crushed
1/4 cup basil leaves or 1
  tablespoon dried leaf basil
  (optional)
1 tablespoon dried leaf
  oregano (optional)
Salt and pepper to taste
1 tablespoon margarine

Trust me. Make this once and you will forever wheel your shopping cart right by the bottled sauces at the supermarket.

Peel and remove seeds from tomatoes. In food processor equipped with the metal blade, process tomatoes 30 seconds, or until pureed. In a large nonstick pan over medium heat, heat olive oil. Stir in onion and garlic. Cook 3 to 5 minutes, or until onion is translucent. Add tomato puree. Add basil and/or oregano, if using. Reduce heat and simmer 5 minutes. With a spoon, remove garlic. Season with salt and pepper. Swirl in margarine. Simmer and stir frequently 20 minutes, or until sauce thickens and is not watery.

All'Italiana: Every Italian family has its own beloved recipe for tomato sauce. This was my family's, and now my daughter Monica serves it to her husband Jean Marc and her little boy Daniel.

Per Serving:
Calories: 245   *Total Fat: 19 g*   *Sat. Fat: 3 g*   *Chol.: 0 mg*

Denise's Vinaigrette

Vinaigrette di Denise

Serves: 6
Preparation Time: 3 minutes
Cooking Time: 0

1 tablespoon red wine vinegar
1 teaspoon Dijon-style mustard
1/4 teaspoon salt
1/4 teaspoon pepper
3 tablespoons olive oil
2 tablespoons water

A recipe borrowed from the French, this is my wife's signature salad dressing. She has never bought a bottled salad dressing in her life—and neither will you once you taste this!

In a salad bowl, combine all ingredients and stir vigorously until blended. Or shake all ingredients in a jar with a tight-fitting lid. Serve with salad greens.

All'Italiana: Make your salad decidedly Italian with arugala, tomatoes, roasted peppers and radicchio.

Per Serving:
Calories: 60   Total Fat: 7 g   Sat. Fat: 1 g   Chol.: 0 mg

Martini Salad Dressing

Salsa al Martini

Serves: 8
Preparation Time: 3 minutes
Cooking Time: 0

1/4 cup olive oil
1/4 cup dry vermouth
1/4 teaspoon salt
1/4 teaspoon pepper
2 tablespoons lemon juice
1 garlic clove, chopped
1/4 teaspoon dried leaf
    marjoram

Shaken or stirred, this is a unique salad dressing— Italians always find an unusual and original way to liven up a recipe.

In a salad bowl, combine all ingredients. Stir until well blended. Or shake all ingredients in a jar with a tight-fitting lid. Serve with salad greens.

All'Italiana: To make a salad an authentic martini salad, include chopped or whole green olives or tiny cocktail onions.

Per Serving:
Calories: 76   *Total Fat: 7 g*   *Sat. Fat: 1 g*   *Chol.: 0 mg*

Chef Dodi's Salad Dressing

Salsa alla Dodi

Serves: 4
Preparation Time: 10 minutes
Cooking Time: 0

1 garlic clove
1 tablespoon red wine vinegar
3 tablespoons olive oil
Pinch of salt
Pinch of pepper
1 tablespoon water

My mother had a bottle of this sitting on the kitchen table every night at dinner. Believe me, the delicate garlic taste helped my brothers, sisters and me enjoy our greens.

In a salad bowl, combine all ingredients. Or shake all ingredients in a jar with a tight-fitting lid. Let stand 5 minutes. Remove garlic and toss with salad greens.

All'Italiana: Be creative—experiment with balsamic vinegar or any Italian herb vinegar you've been wanting to try.

Per Serving:

| Calories: 91 | Total Fat: 10 g | Sat. Fat: 1 g | Chol.: 0 mg |

Dolci

Desserts

Italians don't fancy heavy desserts. The perfect meal is one that ends with a light and subtle dessert. The heaviest dessert I suggest here is Andrea's Tiramisu (page 149), made with reduced-fat cheese and ladyfingers accented with sweet chocolate and the delicate flavor of rich espresso coffee. Other desserts highlight fruits such as pears, lemons or the delicate nutty aroma of almonds. Italian classics such as Spumone (page 152) and Zuccotto (page 151) are made with frozen yogurt or sherbert so dessert lovers can enjoy them in all their authenticity yet without all the fat and cholesterol. Each dessert is so scrumptious, you'll never miss fat and cholesterol-filled ones again. I promise.

Royal Baked Pears

Pere alla Baronessa

Serves: 6
Preparation Time: 20 minutes
Cooking Time: 70 minutes

1 cup water
1/4 cup honey
2 cups sugar
1/4 cup brandy
1 whole clove
2 pinches of salt
6 ripe Bosc pears
1 lemon
2-1/2 to 3 cups amaretto
   cookie crumbs
6 (1-inch-thick) slices lowfat,
   low-cholesterol purchased
   pound cake
6 egg whites

The dessert invented for royalty! These are large servings so serve after a light main course.

In a large pan, boil water, honey, 1 cup of the sugar, brandy, clove and a pinch of salt 5 minutes. Do not boil too furiously. Reduce heat and simmer 15 to 20 minutes, or until mixture becomes a thick syrup. Carefully peel pears. Cut lemon in half and rub pears gently with cut sides of lemon. Place pears in a wide, shallow pan. Pour syrup over pears. If possible to do so without disturbing pears, cover dish with a lid. Simmer over low heat 20 to 25 minutes. Remove from heat and let cool. Preheat oven to 450F (230C). Place cookie crumbs on a plate. Remove pears from pan and set pan with syrup aside. Gently roll each pear in cookie crumbs until coated. Spray a nonstick baking sheet with nonstick cooking spray. Arrange slices of pound cake on baking sheet. Fit one pear onto each slice, pressing them into the softness of the slices for a snug fit. With an electric mixer, beat egg whites and a pinch of salt on high speed 5 minutes, or until stiff but not dry. Reduce speed and slowly fold in remaining 1/2 cup sugar. Using a pastry bag or spoon, pipe or spread pears with an even layer of meringue no thicker than 1 inch. Bake 5 minutes, or until golden-brown. Pour syrup onto individual dessert plates. Arrange each pear with its cake slice in a pool of syrup. Serve at room temperature.

All'Italiana: A recipe borrowed from the French, but one that is loved throughout Italy. Italians traditionally love fruit at the end of a meal.

Variation: Instead of amaretto cookies, use sugar cookie crumbs.

Per Serving:
Calories: 570   *Total Fat: 8 g*   *Sat. Fat: 0 g*   *Chol.: 0 mg*

Andrea's Tiramisu

Tiramisu di Andrea

Serves: 6
Preparation Time: 20 minutes
plus 8 to 10 hours
refrigeration time
Cooking Time: 0

1/2 cup liquid egg substitute
3 tablespoons sugar
1 tablespoon sweet red
    vermouth
8 ounces reduced-fat cream
    cheese, softened
12 ladyfingers
1/3 cup finely ground Italian
    espresso coffee beans
3 tablespoons finely grated
    semisweet chocolate
1/2 cup light whipping cream,
    whipped

My own version of the dessert taking America by storm! First popularized in the San Francisco area, restaurants all over the country are now featuring this remarkably sweet and light treat.

With an electric mixer set at low speed, beat together egg substitute, sugar and vermouth until pale. Stop beating and slowly fold in cream cheese. Fit 6 ladyfingers into the bottom of a 3- to 4-inch-deep serving dish—for the best presentation, use a dish that fits ladyfingers very snugly. Sprinkle with espresso coffee. Gently spread cream cheese mixture on top. Sprinkle with 2 tablespoons of the semisweet chocolate. Arrange remaining 6 ladyfingers across top. Cover with whipped cream. Sprinkle with remaining semisweet chocolate. Refrigerate 8 to 10 hours before serving. Serve cold.

Variation: In the place of whipped cream, nondairy whipped topping can be used.

All'Italiana: The best way to enjoy this dessert is to serve it with a cup of espresso. Even better—pour a snifter of amaretto and luxuriate in the delicate aromas of almond, cocoa and fine espresso.

Per Serving:
Calories: 274   Total Fat: 15 g   Sat. Fat: 9 g   Chol.: 43 mg

Fruit Salad

Macedonia di Frutta

Serves: 8
Preparation Time: 20 to 25 minutes plus 2 to 3 hours refrigeration time
Cooking Time: 0

3 large navel oranges
2 pounds of the freshest fruit you can find: grapes, cherries, plums, melon, etc.
2 McIntosh apples
3 Bosc pears
1/3 cup sugar
3/4 cup cognac
3 bananas
1 quart nonfat lemon, vanilla or plain nonfat yogurt (optional)

In Italian, macedonia means a mixture of many things. This delightful summer dessert is a mixture of some of my favorite fruit.

Zest the peel of 1 orange; set aside. Juice all oranges into a large serving bowl. Cut all fruit except bananas and grapes, if using, into 1/2-inch cubes. If you are using melon, peel and cut into 1/2-inch-thick sections. Add fruit to juice in bowl. Mix in orange peel and sugar. Pour in cognac and mix well. Refrigerate 2 to 3 hours. Mix again gently, making sure orange juice, sugar, orange peel and cognac are blended in well. Arrange slices of banana on top and serve. If serving with yogurt, set a bowl of yogurt on the table for an informal gathering. For a formal party, serve on individual dessert plates with a dollop of yogurt on top or on the side. Serve chilled.

Variation: Maraschino liqueur, peach brandy or banana liqueur can be used instead of cognac to give the dessert a more distinctly fruit flavor.

All'Italiana: Indulge in this quintessential Italian treat and you will end a meal on a sweet, but light and refreshing note.

Per Serving:
Calories: 347   Total Fat: 1 g   Sat. Fat: 0 g   Chol.: 3 mg

Ice Cream Delight

Zuccotto

Serves: 8 to 10
Preparation Time: 30 minutes plus 4 hours freezing time
Cooking Time: 0

1 purchased lowfat, low-cholesterol pound cake
4 tablespoons dark rum
1 pint lowfat vanilla frozen yogurt, softened
2 tablespoons dark rum
1 pint lowfat chocolate frozen yogurt, softened
2 cups nondairy whipped topping

Chocolate Sauce:

1 cup semisweet chocolate chips
1/4 cup finely ground Italian espresso coffee beans
1 teaspoon rum extract
1 tablespoon brown sugar

All'Italiana: Italians love ice cream, and they don't settle for just scoops of it in a dish or cone. They devise wonderful concoctions to serve it up with flair.

Difficult to translate adequately from the Italian, the name zuccotto comes from the word for pumpkin. This dish is made in a mold which resembles a halved pumpkin. I serve it in a loaf pan; it makes things a lot simpler.

Slice pound cake into 1/2-inch-thick slices. Line a 9" X 5" serving dish with plastic wrap, letting ends extend above pan. Line bottom of pan with 1 layer of pound cake slices, cutting to fit. Pour 2 tablespoons of the rum over pound cake slices. Spread the vanilla yogurt over pound cake slices. Add another layer of pound cake. Pour remaining 2 tablespoons rum over pound cake slices. Spread the chocolate yogurt over pound cake and cover completely with whipped topping. Add another layer of pound cake slices on top. Wrap in plastic and freeze 4 hours. About 20 minutes before serving, prepare Chocolate Sauce. Slice Zuccotto into 8 to 10 servings on dessert plates. Serve with sauce on the side or in a bowl for guests to help themselves. Sauce can be served hot, cold or at room temperature.

Chocolate Sauce

In a double boiler over medium heat, combine all ingredients and heat 5 to 10 minutes until chocolate chips are melted and sugar is dissolved.

Variation: Use your favorite frozen vanilla or chocolate dessert, whether it's reduced-calorie ice cream or a tofu substitute for the frozen yogurt. Substitute 24 ladyfingers for pound cake. Also, real whipped cream can be substituted for the nondairy topping.

Per Serving:
Calories: 405   Total Fat: 14 g   Sat. Fat: 9 g   Chol.: 3 mg

Italian Ice Cream

Spumone

Serves: 10
Preparation Time: 30 minutes plus 6-1/2 hours or more freezing time
Cooking Time: 0

2 cups graham cracker crumbs
1 cup chopped candied fruit
1/2 cup chopped almonds
1/2 cup maraschino liqueur
1 cup Tofunetta (page 132)
1 quart vanilla frozen yogurt, softened
1 pint raspberry frozen yogurt, softened
1 pint lemon sherbert, softened

Black Cherry Sauce:
1 cup black cherry jam (Swiss or English preferred)
1/4 cup maraschino liqueur
2 tablespoons water

Traditionally a Southern Italian dessert, I include it because it is one of my personal favorites and because no Italian cookbook, even a Northern Italian one, can be complete without it.

In a medium-size bowl, combine graham cracker crumbs, candied fruit, almonds, liqueur and Tofunetta until well blended. Refrigerate. In a loaf pan, smooth enough vanilla yogurt around the sides and along the bottom to make a 1/2-inch-thick shell inside the pan. Freeze 1/2 hour. Take raspberry yogurt and form a 1/2-inch-thick shell over vanilla yogurt. Freeze 1/2 hour. Finally, line the raspberry yogurt with a 1/2-inch-thick layer of lemon yogurt. Leave enough room in the center to hold crumb mixture. Freeze 1/2 hour. Pour crumb mixture into center. Spread remaining vanilla yogurt across top. Freeze at least 5 hours or overnight. Before serving prepare Black Cherry Sauce. Cut Spumone into 10 slices. Pour enough sauce on dessert plates to cover bottom completely and then arrange slices in middle of sauce. Sauce can also be served on the side.

Black Cherry Sauce

In a medium-size bowl, combine jam and maraschino liqueur. Stir in enough water, a little at a time, to make a smooth, syrupy consistency.

All'Italiana: When I was a kid, the men who sold Spumone wore bright tricolor outfits and carried the wonderful treat in ice chests on their tricycles.

Per Serving:
Calories: 525   Total Fat: 10 g   Sat. Fat: 1 g   Chol.: 6 mg

Sweet Focaccia

Focaccia Dolce

Serves: 8
Preparation Time: 2-1/2 hours
Cooking Time: 20 to 25 minutes

A perfect light dessert or breakfast treat. Think of it as the Italian alternative to doughnuts.

1 cup raisins or chopped candied fruit (or 1/2 cup of each)
1 cup plus 2 tablespoons warm water (110F, 45C)
1 (1/4-oz.) package fast-rise yeast
1 tablespoon granulated sugar
3 cups plus 1 tablespoon all-purpose flour
1/4 teaspoon salt
1/2 cup margarine, softened
1/4 cup packed brown sugar
Finely grated peel of 1 lemon

Soak raisins and/or candied fruit in water 1 hour. Drain, saving water in another large bowl. Reheat to lukewarm. Add yeast and granulated sugar to water. Let stand 10 minutes. Slowly stir in the 3 cups flour, the salt and margarine. Mixture should form a ball, with none sticking to sides of bowl. If dough remains sticky, sprinkle in more flour until dough forms a ball. Blend the 1 tablespoon flour into fruit mixture, then stir mixture into dough. Turn out dough onto a floured surface; knead gently 3 minutes. Spray a 15″ x 12″ nonstick baking pan with nonstick cooking spray. Stretch dough out in pan, cover with a clean towel and let rise in a warm place 1 hour. With your hands, shape focaccia to fit the pan. Cover again and let rise another 30 minutes. About 10 minutes before dough is finished rising, preheat oven to 400F (205C). Sprinkle with brown sugar and lemon peel. Bake 20 to 25 minutes, or until golden-brown on bottom. Cool on a rack. Let stand 1 hour before serving.

All'Italiana: For a special dinner on short notice, I used a Sweet Focaccia prepared the day before and served it with strawberries and zabaglione. It was a hit!

Per Servings:
Calories: 358   Total Fat: 12 g   Sat. Fat: 2 g   Chol.: 0 mg

Italian Crepes

Crespelle

Serves: 6
Preparation Time: 20 minutes
Cooking Time: 15 to 20 minutes

Crepes, see below
Orange Filling, see below
1 tablespoon powdered sugar
1/4 cup Curaçao (optional)

Crepes:
1/2 cup egg substitute
1/3 cup all-purpose flour
1/2 cup skim milk
1-1/2 teaspoons sugar

Orange Filling:
1/4 cup margarine
3/4 cup orange juice
2 tablespoons sugar

Italy adds a twist to a classic French dessert.

Prepare Crepes. Prepare Orange Filling. Dip one crepe at a time in filling until well coated. In the crepe pan over medium heat, cook crepes, one at a time, 2 to 3 minutes, or until liquid is absorbed. With a spatula, fold crepe into a roll and remove from pan. Arrange finished crepes on a serving plate, dust lightly with powdered sugar and serve. If you are adding Curaçao, arrange crepes on serving plate and top with Curaçao, ignite and serve flaming.

Crepes

Combine all ingredients in a medium-size bowl. Using a whisk, mix ingredients until they form a smooth batter. Set aside. Spray a small nonstick skillet with nonstick cooking spray and place over medium heat. Whisk the batter once more, making sure that it is well blended. With a tablespoon, pour enough batter onto pan to make a very thin layer that covers the bottom of skillet. Cook over medium heat 1 minute and turn. Cook 1 minute. Crepes should be light brown. As crepes are done, lay them flat, one on top of the other on a plate. Continue with remaining batter. Set crepes aside.

Orange Filling

In a medium-size pan over low heat, combine margarine with orange juice and sugar. Cook, stirring, 3 to 5 minutes until sugar is melted. Do not boil.

Variation: Instead of using egg substitute, use 6 egg whites.

All'Italiana: This is an ideal Italian dessert—light and delicately sweet. To make it even more authentic, serve with sliced fresh peaches or apricots.

Per Servings:
Calories: 105   Total Fat: 3 g   Sat. Fat: 0.6 g   Chol.: 0.5 mg

154

Cantaloupe Sorbet

Sorbetto di Melone

Serves: 4
Preparation Time: 30 minutes plus 60 minutes freezing time
Cooking Time: 12 to 15 minutes

1 medium-size ripe cantaloupe
2 cups water
About 1/2 cup powdered sugar, or to taste
12 mint leaves (optional)

A rich, frosty dessert that will make ice cream melt with envy.

Cut cantaloupe into eighths. Peel off skin. Cut cantaloupe into pieces. Over high heat, poach cantaloupe in 2 cups boiling water 2 minutes. Drain cantaloupe and discard liquid. In a blender set to high speed or a food processor equipped with the metal blade, process cantaloupe 30 seconds. Stopping the machine, add sugar a little at a time. Taste the mixture as you add the sugar, sweetening to taste. Process until pureed. Transfer into a medium-size freezer-proof container with a lid. Cover and freeze 10 minutes. Transfer into food processor or blender again and process 2 minutes. Again, pour into container and freeze 10 minutes. Remove from freezer and process another 2 minutes. Repeat process of blending and freezing several times until texture of sorbet is firm yet creamy. Sorbet should resemble commercial sherbert in texture. Scoop into individual ice cream bowls. Garnish each scoop with mint leaves, if desired.

All'Italiana: Serve this refreshing dessert like they do in Italy— with store-bought wafer cookies perfect for dipping.

Per Serving:
Calories: 127   Total Fat: 0.6 g   Sat. Fat: 0 g   Chol.: 0 mg

Pears with Meringue Topping

Pere Meringate

Serves: 6
Preparation Time: 20 minutes
Cooking Time: 30 to 35 minutes

6 ripe pears (Bosc or other firm variety)
1/2 cup sugar
1 cup dry white wine
1 teaspoon vanilla extract
5 egg whites

A deliciously light and fluffy dessert, this classic treat makes for an impressive presentation.

Preheat oven to 300F (150C). Peel and core pears. Cut into 1/4-inch crosswise slices. In a large pan over medium heat, bring pear slices, 1/4 cup sugar, wine and vanilla to a gentle boil. Reduce heat and simmer 3 to 5 minutes. Remove from heat and drain pears through a colander. Transfer pears into a shallow baking dish. Gently, smooth surface of pear slices with a spatula. With an electric mixer, beat egg whites until stiff but not dry. Fold in remaining 1/4 cup sugar. Spread egg white mixture over pear slices. With spatula, form small peaks in egg whites. Bake 15 to 20 minutes, or until peaks are golden. Serve warm.

All'Italiana: Try savoring this elegant dessert with Liquore Galliano di Pere, a delicious Italian liqueur.

Per Serving:
Calories: 184   Total Fat: 0.6 g   Sat. Fat: 0 g   Chol.: 0 mg

Lemon Tart

Torta al Limone

Serves: 8
Preparation Time: 30 minutes
plus 30 minutes cooling time
Cooking Time: 45 minutes

Crust, see below
Lemon Filling, see below

Crust:
2 cups all-purpose flour
1/2 cup margarine, softened
5 tablespoons water
2 tablespoons sugar
1/2 teaspoon salt
3 tablespoons vegetable oil

Lemon Filling:
1/2 cup egg substitute
1 cup sugar
Grated peel from 1 lemon
Grated peel from 1 lime
3 tablespoons lemon juice
5 egg whites

A light and sweet dessert perfect for a summer evening .

Preheat oven to 475F (240C). Prepare Crust. Prepare Lemon Filling. Pour into baked pie shell. If quantity of filling is too great for pie shell, save excess and use it as a sauce when serving. Reduce oven temperature to 350F (175C) and bake 20 minutes, or until top is light brown. Let cool on a rack 30 minutes. Slice at the table or, if there is remaining unbaked filling, spoon enough onto individual dessert plates to make a thin layer and place a slice of tart on top.

Crust
In a large bowl, combine all ingredients. Mix well until ingredients form a dough. Turn out dough onto a lightly floured surface. Knead dough gently 3 to 5 times. Roll out dough to 1/4 inch thick. Transfer dough into a 9-inch pie pan. Press dough gently into sides of dish and cut off excess dough that hangs over edge of pie pan. Bake 25 minutes, or until golden-brown. Crust will shrink as it bakes.

Lemon Filling
With an electric mixer, beat egg substitute and 1/2 cup sugar 10 to 12 minutes, or until pale. Fold in lemon peel, lime peel and lemon juice. With an electric mixer in a separate bowl, beat egg whites until stiff but not dry. Slowly fold in remaining sugar. Fold beaten egg whites into egg-substitute mixture.

Variation: Vegetable shortening can be used instead of margarine.

Hint: All filling ingredients should be at room temperature.

All'Italiana: This is a delicious ending to a light meal of pasta or risotto with vegetables, or perhaps a fish entrée. Espresso is the perfect accent.

Per Serving:
Calories: 318   Total Fat: 10 g   Sat. Fat: 1.4 g   Chol.: 0 mg

Almond Cake

Torta di Mandorle

Serves: 8
Preparation Time: 20 minutes
plus 30 minutes cooling time
Cooking Time: 40 minutes

6 egg whites
2 cups powdered sugar
3 cups unsalted, blanched
    almonds, chopped
Grated peel of 1 lemon
1/2 teaspoon vanilla extract
2 tablespoons chopped
    unsalted, blanched almonds

Sit yourself down in a comfy chair with an espresso and enjoy a slice of this delicious cake.

Preheat oven to 350F (175C). Spray a 10-inch round non-stick cake pan evenly with nonstick cooking spray. Dust lightly with flour, turning the pan from side to side to make sure bottom and sides are evenly coated. In a medium-size bowl, beat egg whites until stiff but not dry. Fold in sugar and the 3 cups almonds, alternating between the two. Gently fold in grated lemon peel and vanilla. Pour mixture into pan. Smooth surface with a spatula or spoon. Sprinkle with the 2 tablespoons chopped almonds. Bake 40 minutes or until a knife inserted into center of cake comes out clean. Cool on a rack 10 minutes. Remove from pan and cool at least 20 minutes before serving.

Hint: To blanch almonds: In a large pot over high heat, bring 3 cups of water to a boil. Add 3 cups of shelled almonds and boil 2 to 3 minutes. Drain and cool. When almonds are cool enough to handle, remove skins.

All'Italiana: This cake always takes me back to the times when I sat in outdoor cafés and drank in the fragrant Italian night.

Per Serving:
Calories: 349   Total Fat: 21 g   Sat. Fat: 2 g   Chol.: 0 mg

Italian Recipe List

A

Agnello al Forno 69
Agnello con Ravanelli 68

B

Baccala alla Piancentina 39
Baccala Stoccafisso 38
Brazato di Manzo di Mantova 71
Burro di Acciughe e Sardine 7
Burro di Salmone 8

C

Cannelloni 91
Caponata 13
Caponata alla Siciliana 134
Carciofi Sotto Olio 136
Conchiglie Ortolane 82
Coscia di Montone all'Italiana 67
Cotelette di Maiale alla Vernasca 70
Crespelle 154
Crostacei al Succo Arancia 32
Crostacei in Brodo 33

F

Fagioli Nostrani 123
Fettucine alla Vodka e Salmone 81
Filetto di Tacchino 55
Focaccia Aglio e Cipolla 110
Focaccia Dolce 153
Focaccia Olio e Sale 111
Foglie di Indivia con Burro di Noci 9
Funghi Crudi al Limone e Olio 6

G

Giulienne di Pollo 52
Gnocchi Verdi I 114
Gnocchi Verdi II 115
Gremolata 135

I

Il Vero Pesto alla Genovese 140
Insalata di Fagioli 3
Insalata di Melanzane 5
Insalata di Mozzarella, Pomodori e Basilico 2

L

Lasagne di Pescatore 40

M

Macedonia di Frutta 150

Maionese al Aneto 139

Maionese Rossa 137

Melanzane al Pomodoro Torinesi 128

Melanzane Farcite al Gorgonzola 124

Merluzzo con Pomodoro 31

Minestrone di Andrea 23

Mozzarella in Forno 10

P

Paglia e Fieno al Yogurt 92

Pane di Verdura 112

Pane Zucca 116

Patate alla Rosemarino 126

Penne alla Checca di Porto Santo Stefano 85

Penne con Broccoli e Pangrattato 80

Penne con Melanzane 87

Penne con Salciccia Affumicata 90

Penne con Salsa di Noci 86

Penne Puttanesca 84

Pere alla Baronessa 148

Pere Meringate 156

Pesce al Cartoccio 37

Petti di Pollo al Vermouth 49

Petti di Pollo con Zucca 45

Pisarei e Faso alla Piancentina 113

Polenta al Forno con Fontina 99

Polenta con Broccoli e Gorgonzola 100

Polenta Pasticciata con Ricotta 101

Polenta Semplice 98

Pollo al Dragoncello 44

Pollo al Whisky 50

Pollo alla Cacciatore 46

Pollo Arrosto Alla'Italiana 51

Pollo con Lardo Affumicato 47

Pollo per Tre Giorni 48

Polpette di Tacchino 54

Pomodoro Farciti con Orzo e Salmone 122

Puré di Carote 120

R

Ravanelli Mezzi Cotti 133

Riscotto con Funghi 102

Riso e Fagioli 105

Riso e Zucca 106

Riso Freddo 4

Risotto al Forno 107

Risotto alla Vodka 104

Risotto Milanese 103

S

Salmone e Salsa Verde 30

Salsa al Martini 143

Salsa alla Dodi 144

Salsa di Pomodoro 141

Salsa Verde Piancentina 138

Scallopine di Vitello con Funghi 74

Scaloppine di Vitello coi Peperoni 72

Scarola e Pomodori Amalfitana 127

Scarola Stufata 125

Sedani Brasati 121

Sogliole Infagottate 12

Sorbetto di Melone 155

Spaghetti alla Carbonara 83

Spaghetti alla Checca 94

Spaghetti con le Acciughe 78

Spaghetti e Noci 88

Spaghettini con Tacchino 93

Spigola Arrosto 36

Spumone 152

Sqomberi all Senape e Finocchio 34

Stracciatella 24

Stracotto di Agnello 66

T

Tacchino all Girulia 53

Tacchino all'Americana 57

Tacchino Tonnato 56

Tagliatelle con Ricotta e Noci 89

Tagliatelle con Tonno e Piselli 95

Tiramisu di Andrea 149

Tofunetta 132

Torta al Limone 157

Torta di Mandorle 158

Trota con Funghi 35

U

Uove al Pomodoro in Forno 58

Uove e Porri 61

Uove Farcite Con Peperone 59

Uove Farcite Mantovane 60

Uove Sformate Fiorentine 62

V

Vinaigrette di Denise 142

Vitello Picata 73

Z

Ziti con Salsa di Tacchino in Forno 79

Zucchini con Pangrattato 11

Zuccotto 151

Zupa di Cipolle e Zucche 21

Zuppa di Carote e Tofunetta 18

Zuppa di Cavolo Nero 22

Zuppa di Ceci 19

Zuppa di Giulia 25

Zuppa di Peperoni 17

Zuppa di Piselli 26

Zuppa di Ravanelli 20

Zuppa di Riso e Ceci 16

Index

A

Almond Cake 158
Anchovies, Spaghetti with 78
Anchovy Sauce, Penne with Spicy 84
Anchovy Spread, Sardine & 7
Andrea's Minestrone 23
Andrea's Tiramisu 149
Angel Hair Pasta with Turkey 93
Appetizers & Salads 1-13
Artichokes Braised in Oil 136

B

Bacon, Chicken Roasted with Lean 47
Baked Egg Whites in Tomato Shells 58
Baked Eggplant with Gorgonzola 124
Baked Leg of Lamb 69
Baked Mozzarella 10
Baked Pears, Royal 148
Baked Polenta with Fontina Cheese 99
Baked Polenta with Ricotta 101
Baked Rice 107
Basic Polenta 98
Basil & Garlic, Penne with Tomato, 85

Basil & Yogurt, Spaghetti with Tomato, 94
Basil Salad, Mozzarella & Tomato 2
Bass, Roasted Striped 36
Bean Salad with Tuna, Italian 3
Beans, Rice & 105
Beef, Braised Brisket of 71
Beef, Lamb, Pork & Veal 65-74
Black-Eyed Peas 123
Braised Brisket of Beef 71
Braised Celery 121
Braised Escarole 125
Braised in Oil, Artichokes 136
Bread Crumbs, Penne with Broccoli & 80
Bread Crumbs, Zucchini with 11
Bread Dumplings, Piancentina Style 113
Bread, Garden 112
Bread, Pumpkin 116
Breast of Turkey 55
Broccoli & Bread Crumbs, Penne with 80
Broccoli & Gorgonzola Cheese, Polenta
  with 100
Broth, Scallops in 33
Burgers, Turkey 57

C

Cake, Almond 158
Cantaloupe Sorbet 155
Carrot Puree 120
Carrot Soup, Creamy 18
Celery, Braised 121
Cheese, Baked Polenta with Fontina 99
Cheese, Polenta with Broccoli & Gorgonzola 100
Chef Dodi's Salad Dressing 144
Chicken Breasts with Vermouth 49
Chicken, Drunk 50
Chicken Fingers, Italian 52
Chicken Roasted with Lean Bacon 47
Chicken with Butternut Squash 45
Chicken, Hunter's 46
Chicken, Italian Style, Roasted 51
Chicken, Tarragon 44
Chicken, Three-Day 48
Chickpea Soup 19
Chickpea Soup, Rice & 16
Classic Florentine-Style Baked Eggs 62
Classic Tomato Sauce 141
Cod Fish Pâté 38
Cod with Tomatoes 31
Cod, Piancentina Style, Dried Salted 39
Cold Rice Salad 4
Creamy Carrot Soup 18
Crepes, Italian 154

D

Denise's Vinaigrette 142
Desserts 147-158
Dill Mayonnaise 139
Dressing, Chef Dodi's Salad 144
Dressing, Martini Salad 143
Dried Salted Cod, Piancentina Style 39
Drunk Chicken 50
Dumplings, Piancentina Style, Bread 113
Dumplings, Spinach I 114
Dumplings, Spinach II 115

E

Egg Whites in Tomato Shells, Baked 58
Eggplant Appetizer 13
Eggplant Salad, Italian 5
Eggplant with Gorgonzola, Baked 124
Eggplant with Tomatoes 128
Eggplant, Penne with 87
Eggplant, Sicilian Style 134
Eggs Prepared with Leeks 61
Eggs Stuffed with Red Pepper 59
Eggs with Tangy Filling 60
Eggs, Classic Florentine-Style Baked 62
Endive Leaves, Stuffed 9
Escarole with Tomatoes 127
Escarole, Braised 125

F

Fennel in Mustard Sauce, Mackeral with 34
Fettucini with Salmon, Spiked 81
Fish & Shellfish 29-40
Fish in Parchment 37
Fish Pâté, Cod 38
Fish Rolls 12
Focaccia with Garlic & Onions 110
Focaccia with Olive Oil & Salt 111
Focaccia, Sweet 153
Fontina Cheese, Baked Polenta with 99
Fruit Salad 150

G

Garden Bread 112
Garlic & Onions, Focaccia with 110
Garlic, Penne with Tomato, Basil & 85
Garnish, Simple Radish 133
Genoa Pesto Sauce 140
Gorgonzola Cheese, Polenta with Broccoli & 100
Gorgonzola, Baked Eggplant with 124
Green Sauce, Piancentine Style 138
Green Sauce, Salmon with 30
Greeting viii

H

Ham & Yogurt, Spinach Tagliatelle with 92
Hunter's Chicken 46

I

Ice Cream Delight 151
Ice Cream, Italian 152
Italian Bean Salad with Tuna 3
Italian Braised Leg of Lamb 67
Italian Breads & Dumplings 109-117
Italian Chicken Fingers 52
Italian Crepes 154
Italian Eggplant Salad 5
Italian Ice Cream 152
Italy Does Tofu 132

J

Julia's Soup 25
Julia's Special Turkey 53

L

Lamb with Turnips 68
Lamb, Italian Braised Leg of 67
Lamb, Leg of 66
Lamb, Baked Leg of 69
Lasagna, Seafood 40
Leeks, Eggs Prepared with 61
Leg of Lamb 66
Lemon & Oil, Mushrooms with 6
Lemon Tart 157

M

Mackeral with Fennel in Mustard Sauce 34
Martini Salad Dressing 143
Mayonnaise, Dill 139
Mayonnaise, Red 137
Meatballs, Turkey 54
Meringue Topping, Pears with 156
Milan-Style Rice 103
Milanese Sauce, Special 135

Minestrone, Andrea's 23
Mountain Man Spaghetti 83
Mozzarella, Baked 10
Mozzarella, Tomato & Basil Salad 2
Mushrooms with Lemon & Oil 6
Mushrooms, Rice with 102
Mushrooms, Trout with Porcini 35
Mushrooms, Veal Scallopine with 74
Mustard Sauce, Mackeral with Fennel in 34

O

Olive Oil & Salt, Focaccia with 111
Onion & Squash Soup 21
Onions, Focaccia with Garlic & 110
Orange Juice, Scallops in 32

P

Parchment, Fish in 37
Pasta 77-95
Pasta Shells with Vegetables 82
Pasta with Ricotta & Spinach Filling 91
Pasta with Turkey, Angel Hair 93
Pâté, Cod Fish 38
Pea Soup 26
Pears with Meringue Topping 156
Pears, Royal Baked 148
Peas, Black-Eyed 123
Peas, Tagliatelle with Tuna & 95
Penne with Broccoli & Bread Crumbs 80
Penne with Eggplant 87
Penne with Spicy Anchovy Sauce 84
Penne with Tomato, Basil & Garlic 85
Penne with Turkey Sausage 90
Penne with Walnut Sauce 86
Pepper Soup, Three 17
Peppers, Veal Scallopine with 72
Pesto Sauce, Genoa 140
Polenta & Rice 97-107
Polenta with Broccoli & Gorgonzola Cheese 100
Polenta with Fontina Cheese, Baked 99

Polenta with Ricotta, Baked 101
Polenta, Basic 98
Porcini Mushrooms, Trout with 35
Pork Chops Vernasca 70
Potatoes, Rosemary 126
Poultry & Eggs 43-62
Pumpkin Bread 116
Pumpkin, Rice with 106
Puree, Carrot 120

R
Radish Garnish, Simple 133
Red Cabbage Soup 22
Red Mayonnaise 137
Red Pepper, Eggs Stuffed with 59
Rice & Beans 105
Rice & Chickpea Soup 16
Rice with Mushrooms 102
Rice with Pumpkin 106
Rice, Baked 107
Rice, Milan-Style 103
Rice Salad, Cold 4
Rice, Spiked 104
Ricotta & Spinach Filling, Pasta with 91
Ricotta & Walnuts, Tagliatelle with 89
Ricotta, Baked Polenta with 101
Roasted Chicken, Italian Style 51
Roasted Striped Bass 36
Rosemary Potatoes 126
Royal Baked Pears 148

S
Salad Dressing, Chef Dodi's 144
Salad Dressing, Martini 143
Salad with Tuna, Italian Bean 3
Salad, Cold Rice 4
Salad, Fruit 150
Salad, Italian Eggplant 5
Salad, Mozzarella, Tomato & Basil 2
Salad, Tomatoes Stuffed with Italian Salmon 122

Salmon Salad, Tomatoes Stuffed with Italian 122
Salmon Spread, Smoked 8
Salmon with Green Sauce 30
Salmon, Spiked Fettucini with 81
Salt, Focaccia with Olive Oil & 111
Sardine & Anchovy Spread 7
Sauce, Classic Tomato 141
Sauce, Genoa Pesto 140
Sauce, Piancentine Style, Green 138
Sauce, Special Milanese 135
Sauces & Garnishes 131-144
Sausage, Penne with Turkey 90
Scallops in Broth 33
Scallops in Orange Juice 32
Seafood Lasagna 40
Sicilian Style, Eggplant 134
Simple Radish Garnish 133
Simple Soup 24
Smoked Salmon Spread 8
Sorbet, Cantaloupe 155
Soup, Chickpea 19
Soup, Creamy Carrot 18
Soup, Julia's 25
Soup, Onion & Squash 21
Soup, Pea 26
Soup, Red Cabbage 22
Soup, Rice & Chickpea 16
Soup, Simple 24
Soup, Turnip 20
Soups 15-26
Spaghetti with Anchovies 78
Spaghetti with Tomato, Basil & Yogurt 94
Spaghetti with Walnuts 88
Spaghetti, Mountain Man 83
Special Milanese Sauce 135
Spiked Fettucini with Salmon 81
Spiked Rice 104
Spinach Dumplings I 114
Spinach Dumplings II 114
Spinach Filling, Pasta with Ricotta & 91

Spinach Tagliatelle with Ham & Yogurt 92
Spread, Sardine & Anchovy 7
Spread, Smoked Salmon 8
Squash Soup, Onion & 21
Squash, Chicken with Butternut 45
Stuffed Endive Leaves 9
Sweet Focaccia 153

T
Tagliatelle with Ham & Yogurt, Spinach 92
Tagliatelle with Ricotta & Walnuts 89
Tagliatelle with Tuna & Peas 95
Tarragon Chicken 44
Tart, Lemon 157
Three Pepper Soup 17
Three-Day Chicken 48
Tiramisu, Andrea's 149
Tofu, Italy Does 132
Tomato & Basil Salad, Mozzarella, 2
Tomato Sauce, Classic 141
Tomato Shells, Baked Egg Whites in 58
Tomato, Basil & Garlic, Penne with 85
Tomato, Basil & Yogurt, Spaghetti with 94
Tomatoes Stuffed with Italian Salmon Salad 122
Tomatoes, Cod with 31
Tomatoes, Eggplant with 128
Tomatoes, Escarole with 127
Trout with Porcini Mushrooms 35
Tuna & Peas, Tagliatelle with 95
Tuna Talks Turkey 56
Tuna, Italian Bean Salad with 3
Turkey Burgers 57

Turkey Meatballs 54
Turkey Sauce, Ziti in Succulent 79
Turkey Sausage, Penne with 90
Turkey, Angel Hair Pasta with 93
Turkey, Breast of 55
Turkey, Julia's Special 53
Turkey, Tuna Talks 56
Turnip Soup 20
Turnips, Lamb with 68

V
Veal Piccata 73
Veal Scallopine with Mushrooms 74
Veal Scallopine with Peppers 72
Vegetables 119-128
Vegetables, Pasta Shells with 82
Vermouth, Chicken Breasts with 49
Vinaigrette, Denise's 142

W
Walnut Sauce, Penne 86
Walnuts, Spaghetti with 88
Walnuts, Tagliatelle with Ricotta & 89
Words of Advice ix-x

Y
Yogurt, Spaghetti with Tomato, Basil & 94
Yogurt, Spinach Tagliatelle with Ham & 92

Z
Ziti in Succulent Turkey Sauce 79
Zucchini with Bread Crumbs 11

Metric Charts

Comparison to Metric Measure

When You Know	Symbol	Multiply By	To Find	Symbol
teaspoons	tsp	5.0	milliliters	ml
tablespoons	tbsp	15.0	milliliters	ml
fluid ounces	fl. oz.	30.0	milliliters	ml
cups	c	0.24	liters	l
pints	pt.	0.47	liters	l
quarts	qt.	0.95	liters	l
ounces	oz.	28.0	grams	g
pounds	lb.	0.45	kilograms	kg
Fahrenheit	F	5/9 (after subtracting 32)	Celsius	C

Liquid Measure to Milliliters

1/4 teaspoon	=	1.25 milliliters
1/2 teaspoon	=	2.5 milliliters
3/4 teaspoon	=	3.75 milliliters
1 teaspoon	=	5.0 milliliters
1-1/4 teaspoons	=	6.25 milliliters
1-1/2 teaspoons	=	7.5 milliliters
1-3/4 teaspoons	=	8.75 milliliters
2 teaspoons	=	10.0 milliliters
1 tablespoon	=	15.0 milliliters
2 tablespoons	=	30.0 milliliters

Fahrenheit to Celsius

F	C
200–205	95
220–225	105
245–250	120
275	135
300–305	150
325–330	165
345–350	175
370–375	190
400–405	205
425–430	220
445–450	230
470–475	245
500	260

Liquid Measure to Liters

1/4 cup	=	0.06 liters
1/2 cup	=	0.12 liters
3/4 cup	=	0.18 liters
1 cup	=	0.24 liters
1-1/4 cups	=	0.3 liters
1-1/2 cups	=	0.36 liters
2 cups	=	0.48 liters
2-1/2 cups	=	0.6 liters
3 cups	=	0.72 liters
3-1/2 cups	=	0.84 liters
4 cups	=	0.96 liters
4-1/2 cups	=	1.08 liters
5 cups	=	1.2 liters
5-1/2 cups	=	1.32 liters

About Per Serving Information

The ingredients in each recipe were analyzed for numbers of calories, grams of total fat and saturated fat and milligrams of cholesterol using a nutrient analysis computer program and reference books containing nutrient information. Optional ingredients were not counted in the analysis. The nutrient information is an estimate, because amounts of nutrients will vary, depending on cooking times, freshness of ingredients and the size of vegetables, etc.

About the Authors

Andrea Dodi

Out of a tiny village in Northern Italy grew an enormous passion for food and an unrelenting desire to see the world which would shape Andrea's future. His childhood was spent in poverty, but there always seemed to be food on the table, even if it was simple peasant fare. Andrea learned from his mother and sisters that meals did not have to be made with exotic ingredients or rich sauces to be satisfying. When he was a young man, World War II took him away from his family and left him in a German prison camp. At the end of the war, Andrea had the chance to leave Italy in search of a better life. He found it in Paris. At first he worked in a factory, but soon he was learning how to prepare classic French dishes from some of the most experienced chefs in France. Life in Paris was filled with adventure and new experiences, and before long, he met Denise, the woman who would become his wife. In 1950, Andrea pursued the dream he'd had since he was a boy; he came to America. Denise followed shortly after and the two began to shape their life together and start a family in their new country. Andrea found work as a chef, and before long, his client list read like a who's who in New York, including Irene Selznick, Mary Lasker, William S. Paley and the Heinz family. Throughout the 1960s and 1970s, Andrea continued to be a sought-after chef in New York society. In 1977, he co-wrote his first cookbook entitled *The Cuisine of Venice and Surrounding Northern Regions* (Barron's). In 1983, Andrea and Denise moved to West Palm Beach, Florida where his client list expanded to include Henry Ford II and William Koch, the winner of the 1992 America's Cup. Today, Andrea is semi-retired, but continues to indulge in his love of food while travelling the world as the chef of the America[3] sailing team.

Emily Dodi

Emily's love of food matches that of her father's and after helping to write this book, her culinary skills can now live up to her appetite for delicious, healthy food. No longer limited to grilled cheese sandwiches and tomato sauce from the can, today, she makes her own sauce, and a great one at that. She is a copywriter and lives in Los Angeles.